It Was Unlike Anything
Jennifer Had Ever Known.

It was as tall as a man, walked on two legs, yet its shape and the fur that covered it gave it the appearance of a gigantic wolf. But it was the eyes that were the most terrifying—slanted and green, almost aglow in the starlight. And though there was intelligence behind those eyes, it was unlike anything Jennifer had ever known. This creature was cold, distant. It was impossible to read anything from its eyes save the clear intention to destroy its enemies. A low satisfied growl rumbled from deep in its throat.

It charged straight at Jennifer. . . .

iBooks in the PRIVATE SCHOOL™ Series

#1 NIGHTMARE SESSION
#2 ACADEMY OF TERROR
#3 WITCH'S EYE
#4 SKELETON KEY
#5 THE ENEMY WITHIN
#6 THE LAST ALIEN

Most iBooks are available at special quantity discounts for bulk purchases for sales promotions, premiums or fundraising. Special books or book excerpts can also be created to fit specific needs.
For details, email the publisher
@bricktower@aol.com

PRIVATE SCHOOL
#4

SKELETON KEY

Steven Charles

A BYRON PREISS VISUAL PUBLICATIONS, INC.
BOOK

iBooks
Habent Sua Fata Libelli

iBooks
Manhanset House
Dering Harbor, New York 11965

bricktower@aol.com • www.ibooksinc.com

Library of Congress Cataloging-in-Publication Data
Charles, Steven. Skeleton key.
        (Private School) "A Byron Preiss book."
p. cm.
        [1. Young Adult Fiction—Horror. 2. Young Adult Fiction—Science
Fiction—Alien Contact. 3. Young Adult Fiction—Werewolfs and
                Shifters.] I. Lang, Gary, ill. II. Title. III.
                Series: Charles, Steven. Private School.

ISBN 978-1-59687-733-7
December 2018

SPECIAL THANKS TO RON BUEHL,
PAT MACDONALD, MARJORIE HANLON,
AND DAVID M. HARRIS.
EDITOR—RUTH ASHBY

SKELETON KEY

Table of Contents

One.. 1

Two.. 9

Three..17

Four.. 27

Five.. 35

Six.. 43

Seven.. 51

Eight.. 59

Nine.. 67

Ten..75

Eleven..83

Twelve..93

Thirteen.. 101

Fourteen.. 109

Table of Contents

One

EVENING CAME EARLY WHEN THE CLOUDS SCUDDED in, swallowing the setting sun and filling the gaps between the hills with slow-growing shadows. The air remained dry, but the breeze that slipped down the slope of Ballad Hill touched the campus of Thaler Academy with a vague threat of winter. Many leaves were still at the height of their autumn colors; others were brittle husks that whispered quietly. The tops of the pines dipped slightly, the lowest boughs trembling, and every so often there was the soft rattle of a pine cone falling to the ground.

A truck rumbled past the pillars that marked the academy's main entrance.

A rabbit followed the brick wall that separated the campus from the highway, found its burrow, and popped in just ahead of a nightbird swooping down for its evening meal.

There was no thunder announcing the approach of a storm.

There were only the clouds, slowly shading to black.

The seven main buildings that formed a crescent at the top of the circular drive were lighted here and there, and for the most part they were silent. The library on the second floor of the Student Union was filled with students cramming for examinations, a few classrooms were occupied with after-dinner tutorials, and though the dormitories still had their share of music and laughter, the sounds were muted and short-lived.

In the student and faculty parking lots only a few cars were missing.

Behind the crescent and down a gentle slope, the squat red-brick gymnasium was lighted as well. It was, at night, the best place on campus for letting off steam, and a few girls were on the basketball court playing a frantic game without rules. A few more jogged around the track that circled the floor, and more were settled in the gymnastics room.

In the central locker room locker doors slammed. There were raucous shouts from the showers.

Beyond the locker room at the back of the building, however, in an addition much newer than the rest of the complex, the Olympic-sized swimming pool was empty. Jennifer Field hesitated for just a moment before walking into the pool area, a thick white towel slung around her neck.

Maybe, she thought as the door hissed shut behind her, this isn't a good idea.

The system that kept the vast room and pool heated made the area feel too warm, uncomfortably humid; yet the white- and green-checkered tiles on the floor and walls were damp and cool to the touch. And where the tiles ended, the domed ceiling began—squares of clear glass speckled with droplets of condensation, not thick enough to keep the night sky from peering in.

Jennifer took a step toward the pool and shivered.

It was silent.

With the locker room door closed, the shouts from the others were cut off, sealed off, and all she could hear were the faint drips of water, the sound of her own breathing, and the light slap of water as the filtration system switched on and off and created wavelets that ran along the sides of the pool.

When she coughed, more for the noise than because she had to, there were echoes.

She swallowed, then padded to the steps leading into the pool at the near corner, slipped the towel off, and dropped it to the floor. She wished there was more light, but once the dinner hour was over and classes were done for the day, there remained only four large bulbs burning in each of the high corners, aimed at the pool itself and leaving deep pools of shadow along the walls. Underwater, evenly spaced and protected by wire mesh, were other lights whose beams were distorted, feeble lights that barely illuminated the checkerboard pattern on the pool's bottom.

The odor of chlorine.

The smell of damp wood from the benches around the walls.

Jennifer breathed deeply and took hold of the aluminum railing that curved down with the steps. The water was slightly chilly, comfortable, and she moved down until it was up to her waist. She stood staring down toward the diving board at the other end.

With one hand she tucked a few stray strands of auburn hair under her bathing cap, hating the rule that required such confinement, then pulled down at the sides of her one-piece maroon swimsuit. She looked over her shoulder at the double doors that led back into the locker room, hoping that someone would join her and at the same time hoping she'd be left alone for a while.

She needed to think.

Her studying was done, and the noise in the dorm had suddenly grown too loud, too intrusive. This was the only place she could think to flee to for peace and a few minutes of undisturbed solace.

She turned to face the wall, backed away slowly, and lowered herself beneath the surface. She came up sputtering and grinning and launched herself backward. No Australian crawl or butterfly stroke that night— just a lazy overhand reach and a fluttery kick of her feet, and she felt the water slip over her shoulders and chest and watched the dome drift along with her as if she were on a slow-moving boat, floating along a tropical river.

She floated then, without moving.

Staring at the faint, rippling reflection of the water on the walls. Stick figures shadow dancing just for her.

Moving again until she reached the far end at last and turned around, still on her back and still concentrating on using just enough energy to keep herself from slipping under.

And once back at her starting point at the shallow end, she stood and rubbed her arms, shook them, shook her legs, and took off a second time.

Stroke and kick, sensing rather than seeing the light above and below her, feeling her tension drain away with the exercise.

For a moment Jennifer was distracted when the under side of the diving board slipped into view. She reached for and found the lip of the pool behind her. She rested, her arms out to either side, taking her weight while her legs fluttered just enough to keep them from drifting downward, not missing a beat when she thought she heard the opening and closing of the door leading directly to the outside.

Though she was in the shadow of the board, the lights above her prevented her from seeing if anyone had come in, and, though she waited, no one came to the pool's edge, no one called out to see who she was.

"Hello!" she called then and blinked at the echoes that filled the room. "Over here!"

When the echoes died, there was nothing.

Oh, no, she thought, and a sudden chill rushed across her bare shoulders to settle in her stomach.

She pulled up the sides of her cap to free her ears, and she listened again. It was possible she had been mistaken, that the noise was just a trick of the muffling effect of the water, her light splashing, and the sound of her heart and rushing blood.

"Hello?"

Echo.

She squinted but could see nothing but the wavering image of water on the tiles and the extra shadows it created.

And she knew then, without seeing a thing, without hearing a thing, that she wasn't alone.

Someone was in there with her.

A brief moment when she thought it might be Marysue or Monica playing a trick on her. Both of her friends knew she was going for a swim. All three of them shared a secret that none of them wanted to keep, yet none was able to tell anyone else. She thought then—she hoped—one of her friends was trying to scare her into thinking that one of *them* had entered the pool building, one of—

Something moved.

Over there, on her right, along the wall by a bench.

She turned slowly and thought she saw a shadow drifting along the wall toward her end of the pool.

"Hey, Beauford!" she said and waited for Marysue to answer.

Again the slight movement, though it might have been one of the ripples.

"Holt?" And she dared Monica to try to hide from her then.

As she backed slowly out from under the diving board, she knew it wasn't either of them.

Her friends wouldn't try to scare her, not then. Neither of them would pretend she was one of *them*, one of the aliens they had discovered, living with the human population of Staines Valley, working on a project that would transform the earth's atmosphere into one they would be able to breathe.

And in so doing would destroy every living thing on the planet.

Something moved.

Quickly she pushed away from the side and sidestroked toward the center of the pool, where she treaded water, turning slowly left, then right, cursing the dim light and cursing the water that slapped at her face, finally reaching up and tearing the cap free from her head and tossing it aside.

The splash the cap made was quiet, but it sounded like a gunshot.

"Hey," she said flatly. "Tell me, who is it?"

A bench scraped on the tiles when someone bumped into it, and Jennifer moved a little closer to the shallow end, fear and anger struggling within her.

Fear because she didn't want to be trapped in there with one of the aliens. They were deadly. They were killers. And they knew she and the others understood their secret purpose.

And anger because she was tired of being scared, tired of jumping at her own shadow, tired of being threatened and unable to do anything about it. When Borden Overbrook and Pauline Klopher, the instructor and the widowed librarian, disappeared mysteriously after finding the aliens' hideaway in the forest, Jennifer's friends had been ready to surrender, to give in, but she had told them she'd had enough.

"Fight," she had said. Even if she had to do it alone, she was going to fight.

The lights went out.

Suddenly there was only the night sky overhead, and below her the dim glow of the underwater bulbs. The reflecting shadows on the walls took on sharper edges, shifting more wildly as her hands stirred up the water.

The diving board creaked.

Jennifer continued to sidestroke toward the shallow end, knowing that if she let herself settle the bottom would be only a few inches below her feet.

The diving board creaked, and when her vision adjusted to the dark, she saw a long, dark shadow climb to the board's center, low and hunched over, its form blending with the dark of the wall behind it.

"Jennifer," it said quietly.

She gasped and continued to move away. The voice was rasping, deep, saying her name and growling at the same time.

"Jennifer."

She swallowed, turned her head from side to side, and realized she was standing up, the water just at her waist. It wasn't coming after her. It was playing with her, and she knew it.

"Jennifer, I see you."

"What—what do you want?" she asked, annoyed that her voice was trembling.

"You," it said.

Back another foot, angling toward the steps in the corner. "What?"

"You, Jennifer," it said, its words barely audible above the splashes she made.

Her right heel struck the bottom step.

Through the closed doors behind her, she could hear the sound of muffled laughter.

The creature remained on the diving board, still deep in shadow.

"I don't know what you're talking about."

A small sound, a sound like the scrape of rough metal over metal. It was laughing.

Then it raised its head, and Jennifer moved up the steps quickly. In the light from below, she saw its wolflike form, the gleam of its fangs and the faint glow of its gray fur, and finally the intense green glow from its evil, slanted eyes.

"You, Jennifer," it said. "I want you."

Two

BLINDLY, JENNIFER SNATCHED UP HER TOWEL AND raced for the exit, her shoulders and spine rigid as she expected the creature to leap snarling onto her back to tear out her throat, leaving her body to be discovered in the morning. Her hands fumbled with the crossbar, slipped off, refusing to take hold.

The creature laughed softly.

A wild look over her shoulder, and she fell against the bar, cursing when it didn't move, sobbing when it finally gave way under her weight. Then, nearly falling, she was through the door and into the locker room, gasping for air, stumbling along the wall, constantly looking back over her shoulder.

The door swung closed behind her.

There were a few voices, loud and laughing, some in the shower area that divided the locker room in half down its center, some in the aisles between banks of red and blue lockers. As Jennifer hurried toward her own, a couple of girls called her name in greeting and asked her how the water was. She smiled stiffly, unable to answer. She looked back, looked ahead, and ducked into her aisle where, suddenly, her legs weakened, forcing her to drop onto the worn wooden bench that stretched down the aisle's center.

To her left were the showers, wide areas of white tile through which one could walk to the lockers on the other side. Steam drifted over the top of the dividing wall, sliding down the tiles, coiling on the tiled floor.

No one was in her section, and she whimpered softly as she gave herself over to the violent chills that struck her in waves. Her teeth chattered, her arms and legs broke out in gooseflesh, and she wrapped the towel tightly around her as if it were a shawl.

It isn't coming, she told herself. It's playing with me. *How do you know?*

It isn't. It could have killed me in there, and it didn't.

When the chills subsided, she stood, swayed for a moment, then yanked her locker open and pulled out her clothes. She stripped off her swimsuit, dressed as fast as she could, and slammed the door shut. A spin on the lock until she felt it catch. Her hair was still wet, but she didn't care. All she wanted to do was get out of there and back to her room to contact the others.

They had to know.

They had to know that she had just been warned again—maybe for the last time.

"Hey, Field!"

Her hand slapped her mouth, stifling a scream, and she turned to see a red-haired, slightly chubby girl in a sweatshirt and jogging shorts step through the showers to her side of the room. Barbara O'Malley's freckled face was gleaming with perspiration.

"Sorry," Barbara said, opening her locker and pulling out a towel. "Did I scare you?"

"Just a heart attack, that's all," Jennifer said with a forced grin. "I didn't hear you coming."

The girl pulled the sweatshirt over her head and stuffed it into the locker. "I know what you mean. Everybody's

been nervous since Overbrook and Klopher disappeared."
She wrinkled her nose in mock disgust, the perspiration
sliding down her fair skin. "Everyone thinks they've been
kidnapped and there's a kidnapper in every corner. Can
you believe it?"

Jennifer nodded as she backed slowly toward the outer
aisle. "Armed guards next, right?"

"I hope not. But the dean says we shouldn't go anywhere alone for a while." Barbara laughed. "In packs. Like
wolves."

"That's—great," Jennifer said.

"Hey, if you hang around a minute until I shower, I'll
walk back with you. We can protect each other from the
mad murderer."

"No, that's okay," Jennifer said. "I've got—it's all right;
there's someone—"

She hurried away, the sound of O'Malley's high-
pitched laughter following her to the exit. With one hand
on the crossbar of the heavy metal door, she paused and
looked down the length of the room. At the entrance to
the pool. The door was still closed.

"You, Jennifer. I want you."

Then she was outside and running up the narrow walk
toward the main buildings and dorms. She shivered as
much from the cold as from fright and ordered herself not
to look to either side as she ran. There were only shadows
around her. Only shadows. Nothing to see. Look straight
ahead and keep running.

Once she reached the first building she relaxed, slowed
to a trot and finally to a walk. There were other girls here,
standing in the doorway to the Student Union, walking
from the Union to their dorms. And by the time she
pushed open the door to her own dorm on the far end,
her fear had calmed enough to let her feel anger again.

Up the stairs then, to the back, to her corner room.

The door locked behind her.

From a low chest of drawers set into an alcove on the righthand wall she pulled out a thick towel and scrubbed her wet hair, taking deep breaths, hearing again the voice of the alien answering her, echoing, taunting her, and at the same time warning her that they could reach her whenever and wherever they wanted.

She wasn't safe—not there, not anywhere.

When her hair was as dry as it was going to get with the towel, she stood in front of her dresser mirror and pulled a brush through it, mindlessly, deliberately not thinking until she was done. Then she unlocked her door and crept out into the hall, turned left, and headed for Marysue Beauford's room.

The door was open.

She poked her head in and saw the girl from Virginia sitting at her desk, notebook open, textbooks strewn across the desktop and on the floor beside her. Jennifer knocked on the door frame, and Beauford turned, her smile fading when she saw the look in Jennifer's eyes.

"What?" Marysue asked. "What is it? You look terrified."

"I saw another one," she said, coming in and closing the door behind her.

"When?"

"I was down at the pool and I saw one."

Marysue started to get up, fell back into her chair, and shook her head slowly. "You're sure?"

"It talked to me."

"I'm dreaming, right, Field? This is a nightmare, and any minute now you're going to wake me up and tell me it's time to get to class."

"I wish it was."

Marysue groaned. "I knew it. I knew they wouldn't go away if I pretended they weren't here." A long, loud sigh, and she said, "Tell me."

Jennifer dropped onto the bed, hands clasped between her thighs, and told what had happened, what the alien had said to her, and what she thought it meant. "We haven't got any more time, Marysue. We have to do something, and do it now."

Marysue turned her chair around and raked her hands through her long black hair. "What?" she asked. "What can we do?"

Jennifer looked at her without raising her head. "I have an idea."

"Oh, no," Marysue moaned. "Not another one."

Jennifer almost smiled as she pulled at a strand of hair straggling over her shoulder. But it was true—over the past two days, since the disappearance of Overbrook and Klopher, she had been trying to think of a way to get an adult, someone with authority, to go with them to the alien hideaway they had discovered in the woods beyond Ballad Hill. Just telling someone wouldn't do—no one would believe them—and it was beyond them to bring one of the aliens themselves—they were too strong, too clever, too adept at passing for humans.

"The cops," she said.

Marysue only stared.

"We have to get the cops. We have to convince them to come with us. It's the only way."

"You're nuts."

She shook her head. "No. If the cops could see what we saw, our problems would be over."

"You have a fever," Beauford told her. "Or you're hysterical. Field, we've been over this a hundred million times, and you *know* they aren't going to believe us. The only ones who did were Overbrook and Mrs. Klopher, and look what happened to them—they've disappeared."

Jennifer massaged her knees slowly, stretched her neck, and finally got to her feet. "I was thinking about Rumbel."

"Who?"

"Rumbel. Remember? He's a cop. Lee and Conrad told us about him."

It took a few seconds, but Marysue finally said, "Sure. But what can he do?"

Jennifer paced to the door, to the desk, and back to the door again. It was probably a very dumb idea, but it was the only one she had.

Lee Fawkes and Conrad Chang, high school students from Staines who took a couple of classes at Thaler, were part of the group that had uncovered the alien plot. Lee had told Jennifer about a policeman, Rumbel, who had a grudge against teenagers. Whenever he could, the man would hassle the teenage population of Staines, whether they were walking, driving, or just standing on a corner waiting for the light to change. Lee called him a movie stereotype—fat and obnoxious.

But Lee assured them the man definitely was not stupid. He knew exactly how far he could push within the limits of the law, and he had never once gone over that line.

Suddenly Marysue's eyes widened, then just as quickly narrowed. "Hey, wait a minute, child, I don't know about this," she said very slowly.

"Are you reading my mind, Beauford?"

"I'm reading your death sentence is what I'm reading," Marysue said.

"But it'll work!" Jennifer insisted eagerly. "All we have to do is find out when he's on the road, then get him to chase us to the alien hideout. Once he sees it, he won't care about us. He'll be thinking about them and what a hero he's going to be."

"I don't think so."

Jennifer hurried over and dropped to her knees in front of her friend. "Marysue, think! It'll work! I know it will!"

"But suppose he's one of them?"

"We'll just use the test on him." The aliens used a device attached to their sides that permitted them to breathe the earth's atmosphere. All Jennifer had to do was contrive to stumble against Rumbel, brushing his side and noting his reaction. They could move on from there. It was simple. Perhaps dangerous. But it was, for the moment, the only way they had to distinguish the aliens from everyone else.

Marysue looked doubtful, but Jennifer's excitement was growing. At least it was a plan. Anything was better than doing nothing.

Jennifer stood and patted Marysue on the shoulder. "Think about it, okay? We can't do anything until the morning, anyway, so sleep on it."

"Right," Beauford grumbled. "I'm supposed to sleep after all this. I haven't slept in weeks, and I may never sleep again."

Jennifer shrugged and left, then stood in the hall for a moment before moving on to Monica Holt's room. There the door was closed, and Monica didn't respond to her knock. She waited a few minutes, passing the time with some girls wandering back from the shower room, from downstairs, from one room to another. Soon she decided Monica wasn't going to return anytime soon. Telling Monica the plan would have to wait.

Back in her own small room she sat at her desk and stared out the casement window toward the hills ranged behind the campus. All she could see, however, was her own reflection shimmering every so often when a gust of wind slammed against the rear of the building.

It'll work, she told herself. It'll work because it has to.

She thought of Lee then and wished he were with her, just to hold her and make her feel safe. After all they had been through together, she didn't know if she loved him. But it was enough, for then, to know that he was as close a friend as she was ever likely to get. That was important. Especially now.

She looked at her books, looked at her notes, and knew she wasn't going to get any studying done. With a sigh she rose, put on her nightgown, turned off the lights, and made sure the door was locked. Then she slipped into bed and lay staring at the ceiling.

Within a few minutes she was asleep, dreaming of the pool and the wolf-creature not letting her out of the water until her strength failed and she sank to the bottom.

Listening to the frantic beating of her heart.

Watching herself struggle to regain the surface.

Seeing a face in the rippling light above.

She snapped her eyes open and sat up, drenched in sweat. Blinking at the sunlight pouring in through the window, she realized that someone was pounding on her door.

She pulled on her robe and unlocked the door, stepping back as Monica Holt pushed in and said, "You'd better get dressed, Field. I just heard that Lee's been arrested."

Three

THE DRIVE INTO STAINES SEEMED TO TAKE FOREVER.

By the time Jennifer had thrown on a pair of jeans and a sweater and had dug her jacket out of the closet, Monica had gotten hold of Marysue, and the three of them ran to the student parking lot where they piled into Monica's white Mercedes.

They knew they would be in trouble for leaving the school so early in the day, but Monica had insisted they go at once and Jennifer concurred. She had no intention of pretending it was going to be an ordinary day as she had in the past in order to prevent others from growing suspicious of her actions.

The battle was about to be joined.

The trip from the hillside campus down into the valley was only a little more than three miles, but she felt as though she were traveling a hundred before the forest fell away and the ground leveled out again.

A hundred miles, and a hundred years.

No one said anything.

Monica, her blond hair covered by a blue baseball cap, hunched over the wheel, clearly wanting to speed but not daring to. Marysue, in a heavy sweater and jeans, her hair tied back in a hasty ponytail, sat in the back and for the first time didn't complain once about Holt's driving. And

17

Jennifer, in the passenger seat, only stared, without seeing, out at the farmland and the old houses that soon formed the outskirts of town.

"I don't believe it," Marysue said at last, pushing forward to rest her forearms on the back of the front seat.

Monica only grunted.

"I just don't believe it. I mean, what could Lee have done?"

"I have no idea," Holt said, slapping her hand on the horn when another car tried to pull out from a side road in front of her. "All I know is what I told you."

Jennifer couldn't even begin to guess what Lee had done, but she felt somewhat ashamed that she wasn't entirely surprised that he had been arrested. Several times in the past Lee had shown her that he wasn't entirely unfamiliar with breaking into houses or hot-wiring cars. A good deal of his past, in fact, was unknown to her, but she had never had occasion to question it before. Not seriously, that is.

This arrest, however, changed things.

The car moved slowly through the short business district, past the Hilltop Diner, the movie theater, and small offices until they reached the park. The police station and town's jail, a new brick and marble building, was on a corner diagonally opposite the center of the four-block-square park. Monica parked on the street in front of the building, pocketed her keys, and waited for Jennifer to move.

"I don't know if I can go in there," she responded to the unasked question. She stared at the entrance, thinking that except for the sign over the double doors, it might just as well have been a real estate office or a clinic. "I don't know."

"Don't be silly," Marysue said gently.

Jennifer smiled weakly, took a deep breath, and pushed open the door. As she waited for the others to join her, she looked up at the sky, which had become overcast. The gray clouds hung low over the valley and added to the chill already in the air.

And while she didn't believe in premonitions, she knew, suddenly, that Lee's arrest had something to do with *them*.

"Onward," Monica said, taking her arm. "Let's go."

They pushed through the doors and found themselves in a short hallway. On the right was a closed, unmarked door. A few yards down, on the left, another door opened into a large room, which a high counter cut in half. Molded plastic chairs were lined up along two walls, and behind the counter were several desks. At two of them policewomen banged away at ancient typewriters. A man with sergeant's stripes on his uniform stood at the counter, scribbling in a large book.

Jennifer hesitated. Monica winked at her and strode to the counter. Waited. Cleared her throat and pushed her cap to the back of her head.

The sergeant put down his pen, closed the book, and looked up. And smiled. "Yes?"

"Get out the keys, Sarge, we want to see a prisoner," Monica said brightly and scowled when Jennifer jabbed her in the back.

"Lee Fawkes," Jennifer said, her voice small and nervous. "I'm—that is, we're friends of his, and we heard that he was in some kind of trouble."

The sergeant, a young man with short brown hair and thick eyebrows that nearly met across the bridge of his nose, looked over his shoulder at a large round clock on the wall. "I think," he said, "he's out by now."

"Out?" Marysue said.

"Sure." And he smiled again. "I don't know where you got your information, ladies, but he's not a prisoner. Never was, as far as I know."

"But he was arrested," Monica insisted, shifting her cap down so that the bill almost covered her eyes. She leaned forward to look at his name tag. "Sergeant Easton, I'm sure he was arrested."

Easton never stopped smiling. "Miss, I'm afraid you have a rotten grapevine." Then he looked at Jennifer, and the smile softened. "There were some questions that needed answering," he said.

"Mr. Fawkes was asked to come in and provide us with some information. That's all."

Jennifer, too astonished to say anything, grabbed Monica and pulled her away from the counter. "Questions?" she whispered angrily. "Who told you he was arrested?"

Monica shrugged. "I got a call from a friend, a guy I know, okay? He said—"

"I know what he said," Jennifer snapped. "What I want to know is—"

"Miss?"

She turned to the sergeant, who nodded toward the door. "Your friend just walked by."

Jennifer ran out of the room, skidded on the tiled floor as she turned, and saw Lee just leaving the building. She raced after him, slapping open the doors and calling his name. He turned, frowning, and his mouth opened when he saw her hurrying down the steps.

"What are you doing here?" he asked.

She jerked a thumb over her shoulder. "I thought—Monica heard that—" She stopped, catching her breath, and forced herself not to throw her arms around his neck.

For his part Lee seemed embarrassed at the attention. His sandy hair was tousled by the wind, his dark leather jacket zipped closed to the neck. And when Marysue and Monica burst from the station as well, he shook his head and looked away.

"What are you guys?" he asked Jennifer, turning back. "The cavalry?"

"We were worried," she answered.

"Oh." Then he took her hand and started to walk with her, but stopped when she resisted and pointed at Monica's car. "No," he said. "Let's walk a little. I have something to tell you."

"You sure do," Marysue said, coming up to them with Monica. "I want to know why you weren't a for-real prisoner."

Jennifer saw a spark of anger flare in his eyes and then saw it fade just as quickly as it had appeared. She hoped he wasn't going to be in one of his moods. Most of the time he kept his temper controlled, and Jennifer loved being with him, but he had moments when he couldn't control either his envy or his distrust of the wealthy Thaler girls. Jennifer didn't count because she was on a scholarship. Marysue had won his approval only because she was a friend of Jennifer and Conrad Chang.

At the first corner, they crossed the street and arranged themselves on a bench in front of the hedge that separated the town park from the street. Traffic was light, the breeze now calm, and a scattering of dead leaves settled beneath their feet.

"I was still in bed," he said, "when Rumbel came."

"Oh, wonderful," Marysue said.

Lee glared at the curb, his shoulders hunched. "He wanted to know where I was last night and the night before that. Seems like there are some guys working the neighborhoods. Breaking in, stuff like that."

"And he came down on you?" Jennifer asked in disbelief.

"Yeah."

"Because I am in polite company," Marysue said in her best southern belle voice, "I will only say that it stinks."

"They didn't keep you though," Monica said.

"Because I was with my dad all last night," said Lee. "I worked late at his store, went home with him, and stayed home." His smile was humorless. "I still don't think Rumbel believes me."

"Maybe you can get him for harassment or something," Beauford said.

"Don't be stupid," Monica told her. "The guy's just doing his job, that's all. Maybe somebody saw someone who looked like Lee."

She didn't flinch when Lee gave her an acid look, and only shrugged when Marysue muttered something to her too quietly for Jennifer to hear.

Then Lee said, "Speak of the devil."

The girls looked across the street and saw a large man leaving the police station. He was in an ill-fitting dark blue suit, his head covered by a battered brown hat, and even at that distance they could see that his face was flushed. He walked with the gait of a man used to carrying too much weight, and in his left hand he was holding a long cigar.

For a moment he stopped and looked at the Mercedes, nodded, peered inside, and nodded again. Then he patted the roof and moved on.

Jennifer sighed silently and shifted when the man made a sharp left turn and walked across the street right for them, ignoring the cars that honked at him, glaring at one that shrieked to a halt only inches from his leg. When he reached the curb, he put the cigar in his mouth and pulled a lighter from his trousers' pocket. As he watched them with eyes nearly buried in folds of fat, he lit the cigar and turned away to blow smoke over his shoulder.

"You're supposed to be in school," Rumbel said, slowly moving his head so he could glare at them. His voice was deep and rough edged.

"We don't have any classes right now," Marysue said politely.

"We're from Thaler," Monica explained.

"Well, he isn't," the man said, pointing the cigar at Lee. "Move on, pal, before you get picked up for truancy. And you three better get back where you belong."

Jennifer felt Lee tense and put a hand on his arm, told him with a glance not to say anything, and slid off the wall. After hesitating, he followed reluctantly and took her hand, and they all headed back toward the car. Beauford and Holt trailed, saying nothing, and when they reached the car, the two girls got in without a word.

Rumbel remained where he was. Watching.

Lee jammed his hands into his pockets and remained standing on the sidewalk, glaring at the pavement. "He's trouble, Jen," he said quietly.

"Good."

He looked at her in bewilderment, and she couldn't help a quick laugh before launching into an explanation of her plan. Lee tried several times to interrupt her, but she wouldn't let him, and when she was finished she glanced over at the cop still standing in front of the hedge.

"He's perfect, Lee, don't you see that? He's just what we want."

"I don't know."

Jennifer took hold of his arm and waited until he looked at her. "He is, Lee, trust me. He's a creep, just like you said, but that's going to work in our favor, see? If we can get him to follow us, we've got it made."

Lee shook his head doubtfully. "Here he comes. I'd better go, or I'll get nailed for vagrancy or something."

"Okay. I'll see you this afternoon. After—" She stopped. She was going to say, "After ecology class," but the still missing Borden Overbrook was their instructor, and they had been told to spend their classtime in the library until further notice.

Lee, however, knew what she meant and nodded. He was about to lean forward to kiss her cheek but changed his mind and moved off in a huriy. She watched him go and sensed Rumbel coming up from behind her.

"He's trouble, you know," the man said over her shoulder.

"I don't think so," she answered stiffly.

"Yeah, he's trouble. Him and his pals, they're in for a lot of surprises if they think they can keep this up. You know what I mean?"

Slowly she turned to look at him, and slowly she shook her head. "No, I don't know," she said. "And I'm sure you're mistaken, officer."

She opened the car door and slid in, but Rumbel took hold of the handle and prevented her from closing it. He leaned over, the cigar jutting from a corner of his mouth, and looked at the girls one by one.

"If you're his friends," he said with a crooked smile, "I guess I'll be seeing you again."

Then he slammed the door and walked off.

And Jennifer nodded.

Whether he would be on their side or not, the battle had indeed been joined.

Four

"I DON'T BELIEVE IT," MARYSUE WHISPERED. THEN, louder, "I just don't believe it!"

Jennifer hurried into the other girl's room and closed the door, leaned against it, and stared straight ahead.

"How," Beauford said, "could we have been so stupid? You'd think we were just born yesterday."

She stood at her desk and gestured furiously at the open books on its top and those spilled onto the floor. She glared at the notebook whose pages had been partially ripped out in someone's haste to flip through them. Then she dropped into her chair and looked at the ceiling.

"I don't care what you say, child, I am calling in the marines."

Marysue insisted that her desk had been searched. And Jennifer had to believe her because she could tell the rest of the room had been gone through too. Each dresser drawer had been opened and the clothes shoved out of place, the bedclothes had been pulled off the mattress, and in the closet all the clothes had been pushed away from the center.

"Y'know," Marysue said, "they didn't—" She took a deep breath and shook her head. "They didn't even *try* to put it all back. They didn't even care whether I knew it or not."

The morning light outside was still gray from the heavy cloud cover, and the shadows in the room were weak and cold. Marysue hadn't bothered to turn on the lamp; it was all too clear what had happened.

Jennifer crossed her arms over her chest and hugged herself against a feeling of dread. She shivered. When they had returned to campus, Monica had told them she would come to the dorm after getting a book from the library. That was nearly five minutes before. And Jennifer was still in Marysue's room, afraid to look in her own.

"They didn't even try," Marysue repeated quietly.

A trick. The whole morning's episode must have been a trick to make sure they were away from their rooms long enough so someone could search them. Jennifer wasn't sure what they'd been looking for, but she could make a fair guess—notes. Her notes, those of Dean Innlake, or those of the missing librarian, Pauline Klopher. Evidence they had collected that proved the aliens existed.

She closed her eyes and leaned back against the door. "So, Field, now what?"

Jennifer didn't say a word. She only opened the door and walked into the hall, looking left before turning in the opposite direction toward her room. When she reached her door, she turned the knob without hesitating, and her expression betrayed nothing when she saw her clothes, her books, and her cosmetics strewn across the floor.

She stepped inside.

Marysue came in behind her.

She picked up a skirt and shook it, took it to the closet, and hung it up.

"Field?"

Methodically, without a word, Jennifer returned the rest of her clothes to their places, then went to work on her books and her desk.

"Jen?"

When that was finished, she motioned Beauford to help her remake the bed, telling her with her eyes that she didn't want to talk. Not yet. Not then. Not until order had been returned could she think without screaming in rage.

And when she was done with the room, she simply said, "Monica," and went straight to Holt's room. Her knock on the door brought no response. Another knock, and then she pounded—no response. When she tried the knob, it wouldn't turn. At that moment Karen Immano hurried by and called over her shoulder that Monica had last been seen heading away from the dorm and the Student Union.

Jennifer clenched her fists and tightened her brow.

"Jenny," Marysue said, "you can't think that again. It can't be."

But Jennifer didn't know what else to think. Only about a week before, she had accused Monica of being an alien and had been proven wrong. Shamefully wrong. But now her doubts were beginning to surface again.

It was possible Holt had actually received that telephone call, the caller knowing the three girls would rush immediately into Staines to see what had happened. If that was true, it was also possible that Rumbel's wanting Lee for questioning was part of the plan to get them off campus.

She shook her head once, sharply.

Too many possibles.

It was also possible that the caller, having seen Lee go into the station, took advantage of a perfect opportunity.

And it was possible there had been no call at all.

Too many, she thought. And too many suspicions.

"C'mon," Jennifer said. "Let's clean up your room and go to lunch. I'm starving."

"Lunch?" Marysue yelped as she followed Jennifer down the hall. "How can you think of eating when we've been burgled, or robbed, or whatever?"

"Nothing was taken, right?"

Marysue nodded. The first thing she'd done was check her jewelry, and not a piece was missing.

"Then what do you suggest? We call the police and tell them our rooms have been searched? They'll ask why. We don't have an answer they'll believe." She shrugged sadly. "I don't see what else we can do."

"We can tear Holt's face off, for one thing," Marysue said angrily.

Jennifer laughed. "We don't know for sure," she said without much enthusiasm.

"I guess," Marysue admitted after a second's hesitation. "But it would be nice. Then I'd have a good reason for hating her."

They worked swiftly in Marysue's room, with Marysue muttering and swearing the entire time. When they were done, they grabbed their jackets and headed for the dining hall in the Student Union.

Neither girl mentioned what had happened to anyone. They scanned the crowded tables and exchanged glances when they couldn't see Monica Holt.

The food was tasteless, the noise and chatter unbearable, and Jennifer ate as quickly as she could, paying hardly any attention to those who tried to talk with her. She knew that she didn't dare lose her temper then. She had to remain calm. Otherwise, she would act without thinking, and she imagined that that was exactly what the aliens wanted.

They wanted her to panic.

They wanted her to isolate herself in some way, and then they would move in.

Earlier, at the beginning of the nightmare, she had convinced herself the creatures wouldn't harm her because to do so would call too much attention to the academy. They had already disposed of one student. If any others disappeared, someone was bound to investigate.

Now things were different.

Jennifer knew where the aliens' base was.

She knew what they were planning.

They could no longer afford to leave her alone, just as they could not have left the former dean, John Innlake, alive when, as she'd speculated, he'd threatened to expose them when his association with them had gone sour.

Moving like a robot, she returned her tray and walked out to the front of the building, pausing only long enough to glance into the Unon's game room. It was empty.

Marysue followed her, her cheeks pale, her hands tugging constantly at her ponytail until she pulled too hard and uttered a short curse. They watched the movement of students across the grassy insert of the circular drive; they listened to the giggles, the laughs, the snatches of gossip and argument that swirled around them; and when they saw the white Mercedes glide between the pillars that marked the academy's entrance, Marysue slapped her arm.

"That's it," she said. "C'mon, Field."

Puzzled, Jennifer followed her back into the Union, where she marched directly to a bank of public telephones beside the bulletin board. Cadging some change, Marysue dialed a number, turned her back, and began talking.

Jennifer could only watch, catching one short, barked sentence: "I don't care how much it costs, just bring it out here!"

Beauford slammed the receiver back onto its cradle and grinned. "The old red machine will be here in an hour."

Jennifer gaped. "But it's—"

"Finished, or darn near," Beauford said, taking Jennifer's arm and pulling her back outside. "The jerk was going to wait for me to come into town to get it. Can you imagine? I could've been waiting here until graduation before he found the brains to let me know."

The red machine was Marysue's old, full-sized Thunderbird, a legacy from her brother and a car that, though lovingly cared for, had seen better days. It had been in a Staines garage for a few days being worked on, but Marysue had evidently promised the mechanic quick money for a personal delivery.

When she asked about it, Marysue grinned and answered in an exaggerated southern drawl. "Well, sure, honey, I promised him a big tip. What's the sense of having the stuff if you can't spend it, huh? I don't intend to line my coffin with it when I go. What a waste!"

Jennifer didn't know what to say. The Beaufords were a wealthy Richmond family; the Fields were solidly middle class. Yet Marysue had never once made a point of acknowledging that difference in their backgrounds. In fact, except for moments like this, Jennifer seldom thought about it herself.

"Besides," the girl continued, "it's in a good cause, right? We can't trust ol' Monica now, not until we find out if she told the truth."

Again Jennifer felt torn between her new suspicions and the results of the old ones. But she also understood that now she was in a fight for her life.

"So!" Marysue said. "What next?"

Jennifer thought a moment, then crossed down off the porch of the Student Union and into a stream of students hurrying to their next classes. "We still don't know about Overbrook, right? All we know is that he's gone."

"Dead, most likely."

"No!" she snapped. "We can't think that, Marysue. Why don't we snoop around a bit until Lee and Conrad get here?"

"And if we get caught?" Beauford asked.

"We'll deal with it then."

"Wonderful. So—where?"

"Overbrook's lab."

And though there was no reason for anyone to stop them, Jennifer couldn't help feeling as if everyone was watching as they hurried up the steps into the science building and took the staircase down into the basement, which consisted of a warren of rooms and labs reaching out beyond the aboveground walls. Some of the rooms were in use, and Jennifer was somewhat comforted by the muted sounds of instructors and students talking. But that security died as soon as she reached the door to Borden Overbrook's lab.

He laughingly called it the dungeon because it was stuck off in a corner all by itself. It was small, empty, and dimly lit. Only the globes in the hall ceiling were on. Vials, jars, and cartons were stacked on the shelves; books were piled on the man's desk; and the lab tables looked as if they hadn't been used in years.

"Creepy," Marysue said and immediately volunteered to stand at the door in case someone interrupted them.

Jennifer didn't argue. Knowing full well she probably wouldn't find a thing, nevertheless she tackled the desk drawers, the books, the shelves, even the storage closets at the back of the room. An hour later, just as the other labs were taking a break and the halls were filling with students, she admitted defeat.

"Hopeless," she said, closing the door behind her. "Now if we could only get into Mrs. Klopher's apartment. Maybe we could find something—"

"Whoa!" Marysue said, hands up, shaking her head. "No way, child, am I going to break into a faculty boarding-house. No way at all. If you do that, you are on your own."

Jennifer opened her mouth to argue but changed her mind when she saw, at the end of the hall, Esther Fine starting up a set of stairs.

"I've got it!" she said and began running.

"Got what?" Marysue demanded and saw where she was looking. "Esther? You want to talk to Esther?"

"Klopher," she said.

"Klopher?" Marysue asked.

"Seeing Esther reminded me of Klopher."

Jennifer shook her head and ducked into the first stairwell she reached. As she took the stairs two at a time, she berated herself for not thinking of it sooner. Mrs. Klopher's apartment had already been searched by the aliens. But the last time Jennifer had seen Mrs. Klopher, the woman had implied that the notes she had made weren't easy to get hold of.

Which meant they probably weren't in her rooms.

Which meant, Jennifer hoped, they were where no one would think to look for them—in the library.

Five

THE OVERCAST SHEET OF GRAY HAD DEEPENED AND reached down lower over the hills while they were inside. Tendrils of cloud drifted over the summits as the girls hurried out of the building and turned toward the Student Union. The temperature, too, was lower, and Jennifer could imagine that before the day was over they could have the season's first flurries. Ordinarily snow would have excited her; now it only depressed her, because if it was true, it would mean getting around would be all that much more difficult. It was much too early in the year for snow, she thought suddenly. Maybe *they* were doing something to change the weather too.

They had just reached the Union entrance when suddenly Marysue slapped her shoulder.

"What?"

"My baby has come home to roost!" Beauford shouted and ran toward the drive.

Jennifer watched Marysue, wondering what had gotten into her, until she saw the familiar bullet shape of the red Thunderbird coming up the long drive. She looked at the doors in frustration, debated, then ran after her friend, grinning broadly as Marysue jumped onto the blacktop and waved her arms frantically to stop the mechanic. Then she ran around to the driver's side, practically yanked the driver out, and sat behind the steering wheel, caressing it with one palm while she adjusted the rearview mirror with the other.

Jennifer looked at the man, who seemed only a few years older than Lee, and said, "She's missed it."

He nodded without smiling, reached into his coveralls pocket, and pulled out a crumpled sheet of paper, which he handed to Marysue through the window. "All listed," he said. "Including the special delivery."

Marysue laughed, grabbed the bill, and climbed out, asking him to wait. Then she sprinted for the dorm, waving the paper over her head.

"She always get that way over this car?" the man asked, pushing a stained hand back over his short-cropped hair.

Jennifer leaned back against the fender and shrugged. "I guess so." The name *Chuck* was embroidered on the coveralls, and Jennifer tried not to smile when she saw Chuck notice that the campus was crawling with young women, and only young women. "You don't get up here much?"

He shook his head slowly.

"Did you have trouble fixing the car?"

"Nope," he said absently. "Would've been quicker if she didn't keep calling all the time."

She did smile then. "It's a family heirloom."

Finally he looked at her, frowning as though trying to decide if she was joking. "Good car. She sure beats the heck out of it, though."

Jennifer was saved from saying anything more by the return of Marysue, checkbook and pen in hand. They went over the bill, and Marysue saw for herself that everything was in order. Then she wrote out the check, handed it to the mechanic with a flourish, and winked at Jennifer when the young man's eyes widened.

"Too much," he said.

"For your trouble," she answered. "Now get in. I'll drive you back to town."

"Hey, Marysue," Jennifer said.

"Don't worry about it," Beauford said as she jumped into the car. "I'll be back before you know it. You want to come? See how she runs?"

"No. I'll—I guess I'll wait."

"Okay," Marysue said, barely able to contain her pleasure at having her car back. "Look, I'll—I'll see if I can give the boys a lift. With Conrad's heap all smashed up, he'll have to walk or hitch or ride on the back of Lee's bicycle. I'll probably see them on the way."

Jennifer wanted to protest, to remind Marysue of what they were supposed to be doing, but Chuck was listening, and all she could do was nod glumly.

"Don't worry," Beauford said then. "Another half an hour isn't going to make all that much difference."

"Sure. Okay."

She backed quickly out of the way as Marysue shot forward, barely giving the mechanic a chance to close the door. And with the horn honking and the sound of Marysue's delighted laughter fading away, Jennifer puffed up her cheeks, blew out a breath, and decided just then to check the library on her own.

The odds of her finding anything, she knew, were small to nonexistent, but until Lee and Conrad showed up for their afternoon classes, there wasn't much she could do alone, and she was too impatient simply to wait.

The library took up the entire second floor of the Student Union. Jennifer stood on the landing outside the open doors, looking in at the students drifting among the stacks, jockeying for places at the tables in the center of the room.

Jennifer waited almost a full minute before going in, and upon entering she was immediately struck by the silence that greeted her. There were whispers, of course, the snap of pages turning, the scuffing of feet, and the occasional shriek of a chair being pushed back, but other than that the place could have been deserted. To her right was a small horseshoe-shaped desk, and behind it sat a dark-skinned girl whose name she knew but couldn't recall. A senior. From someplace out west. Became a student librarian not for the money but for the chance of putting it on her record, for college.

Then she remembered and walked over.

"Hi, Tami."

Tami Nells looked up at her from under a row of thick, black bangs. "Hi."

"Looks busy."

Nells grimaced and looked away pointedly. There was a book open in front of her, and, Jennifer saw, keys lying beside it.

"You ought to take a break," she said, as sincerely as she could. "You must've been here all day, what with Klopher gone and all."

Nells, still scowling, looked up. "Yeah. And no one would cover for me at lunch. Fine had a class, so she said."

Jennifer pretended to think for a minute before saying, "Well, I'll cover for you if you want to run downstairs for something to eat."

Suspicion instantly clouded the girl's face, but Jennifer maintained her expression—the innocence of a newcomer who wanted to make points with the seniors. A moment later Nells nodded her decision, slammed her book closed, and walked around to the front of the desk.

"Just don't do anything, okay?" she ordered. "You screw something up, it's my fault, got it?"

"Hey, no problem," Jennifer said, taking Tami's place on the tall stool and folding her hands on the desk. She narrowed her eyes in a glower. "I'll just pretend I'm Klopher."

She almost received a smile, got a grunt instead, and, as soon as Nells was out the door, Jennifer started opening drawers. Slowly. As though she knew what she was looking for.

There were four on either side of her and one in the center. The center one contained nothing but rubber stamps, paper clips, and other supplies. The drawers on the left, all of them unlocked, held papers and forms, a few books, and file folders.

The two top drawers on the righthand side were the same.

A pair of freshmen approached her, and she apologized when she was unable to answer their questions. "Just filling in for a while," she said, assuring them that the regular girl would be back any minute.

The third drawer was locked, and she quietly picked up the keys and opened it. Nothing but a metal box. She glanced around the room, smiled absently in case anyone was watching, and reached down to open the box. There was money inside. Fines, she concluded, for overdue books.

The bottom drawer had a label on it, so worn she had to lean down to read it: PRIVATE.

Bingo, she thought. She crossed her fingers and tried three keys before locating the right one.

Then she sat up, checked the room and doors again, and reminded herself that there was probably nothing in there she could use. Surely the aliens had already searched the desk, and if there had been anything in there before it would be gone now.

She turned the key, pulled it out, and replaced the keys on the desktop where she had found them.

And someone spoke her name.

Hoping she didn't look as guilty as she felt, she saw Barbara O'Malley standing in front of her, a pair of books cradled in one arm.

"Hi, Field. I want to take these out."

Jennifer explained a second time that she was only sitting in for Nells, and O'Malley rolled her eyes.

"You know, this is a royal pain in the—"

"Wait a minute," Jennifer said, forestalling what she knew would be a long string of inventive curses, for which O'Malley was well known. The girl had tried them out on an instructor once and had spent most of the previous spring term on probation.

Barbara closed her mouth and sighed. "Okay, I'll wait." And when she looked as if she were going to wait right at the desk, Jennifer smiled apologetically at her and opened the book Nells had left behind, making a great show of studying the first page she came to.

At last O'Malley took the hint and stomped off, muttering loudly.

Jennifer grinned to herself but didn't look down at the drawer. Too many people were drifting across the front of the room right then, and she began to worry that Nells would return before she had a chance to check the last one.

Stupid, she told herself. This is stupid. If you get caught, what are you going to say?

The room finally settled down.

And after taking a deep breath, she slid the drawer open.

It was empty.

She pulled it out as far as it would go, tugging once when it got stuck, and closed her eyes briefly in disappointment. No miracles here, Field, she told herself. She started to close it, frowning when it got stuck a second time.

It was probably nothing.

But with nothing to lose, she slipped off the stool and knelt beside it. When she leaned over to peer into the back, she saw nothing that could have caused the obstruction, but when she pulled the drawer toward her again she was positive she felt and heard paper crumpling. Feeling as if everyone in the library was watching her, she felt along the underside of the drawer until, with a gasp she couldn't contain, her fingers brushed across the unmistakable bulk of an envelope.

Oh, no, she thought and yanked at it several times before the tape pulled free.

She turned it over once, starting to look at it, but changed her mind and closed the drawer. Once back on the stool, she slipped the envelope into the pocket of her jacket, which she had never removed, and began looking at her watch.

In fifteen minutes she would have to be back outside. Until then, or until Nells returned, she didn't dare open the envelope in case someone saw her do it.

Time dropped to a maddening crawl.

And ten minutes later, just as she was about to get up and look out the door for Tami, Dean Dramon walked into the library. Jennifer couldn't help but stare. He was a tall, darkly handsome man who had a fair percentage of the student body lusting after him, dreaming about him, and deathly afraid of him because of his strict insistence on their obeying not only the letter but also the spirit of the academy's rules.

He was wearing a black suit, a blue open-neck shirt, and a burgundy cashmere muffler draped casually around his neck.

Jennifer hoped he wouldn't look at her, and when he did it was all she could do not to leap up from her stool and bolt for the door.

"Miss Field," he said with a smile.

"Dean Dramon."

"I didn't know you worked here."

"Just sitting in for a while," she said and nervously rubbed her palms against her knees once. "TamiNells ought to be back—"

But the dean had already turned away, beckoned to Barbara O'Malley, and stood waiting with his hands clasped behind his back. Jennifer ignored the frantic look the girl gave her. All she wanted now was to get out of there. But the dean didn't move away when O'Malley joined him; he only leaned forward and whispered something in her ear. Barbara's eyes widened, and she nodded quickly, then dumped the books she was carrying onto the desk and ran for the stairs.

The dean turned to watch her go.

Then he looked at Jennifer and said, "When you're through playing games, Miss Field, I'll see you in my office."

Six

DRAMON SMOOTHED THE BURGUNDY MUFFLER along his chest as if he were adjusting his lapels. A last glance at the library, and he left without looking back.

The noise level in the room rose perceptibly.

The temperature appeared to drop.

Jennifer didn't know what to do. She did clamp an arm against her side to feel the bulk of the envelope in her pocket. The urge to open it was over-whelming now, but as long as the dean was still around, she didn't dare.

For weeks she had known, without tangible proof, that the man was somehow connected with the aliens. Whether he was actually one of them or simply working with them she hadn't been able to determine, but she had received ample clues and enough veiled threats not to be mistaken about her supposition.

She forced herself not to look at the doors in case he was standing off in the shadows watching her.

The expression on his face reminded her of the alien that had confronted her in the pool.

Her breathing grew shallow and rapid, and she leaned forward on her elbows, covering her eyes with her hands, praying for an earthquake, a tornado, any disaster to save her from having to see the man again, alone.

Marysue, she thought, *please hurry back!*

And when Tami returned, complaining bitterly about the food in the vending machines, Jennifer smiled quickly at her and hurried to the landing, where she braced herself against the metal railing to look down into the Union foyer. Dramon was nowhere to be seen, and she took the stairs down slowly, cautiously. At the bottom she froze.

The dean was standing just outside the main door, chatting with a group of girls.

She couldn't go out that way. She just couldn't meet him and go to his office. Had he mentioned something about her grades, or her spending too much time off campus lately, then she would have obeyed. Reluctantly, but she would have gone.

But he had said, "When you're through playing games," and to her that could mean only one thing.

Keeping a careful eye on the man's back, she moved toward the double swinging doors to her left just beyond the dining hall. Beyond the doors lay the clinic, some storerooms, and the bookstore. At the end of that hall was an exit to the lawn behind the crescent, and if she could get there without being spotted, she might be able to make her way around to her dorm to find Marysue and Lee.

Just then, a large group of chattering students burst out of the gameroom and headed for the front doors. She moved swiftly into the hallway, using them for cover. As soon as the doors swung shut behind her, she slowed down, put a hand to her chest to keep her heart from leaping out, and tried to appear as if she knew where she was going and didn't have time to stop and chat.

On the right, the bookstore was open, but no one saw her pass. Farther down, the door to the clinic was open, and there were two girls sitting in the molded plastic chairs, waiting for someone to take care of them. It wasn't unusual—the twenty-four-hour flu managed to strike with remarkable regularity.

A nervous glance over her shoulder only a few yards from the exit made her stop. The dean had come to look for her. Through the glass in the top half of the hall door, Jennifer could see his profile. He was slowly turning to look down the hall, and he'd see her as soon as he turned all the way around.

Looking around in near panic, she saw a half open door on her left and, without thinking, lunged through it and pulled it closed.

It was dark.

She groped along the near walls until she found a light switch, flicked it on, and, startled, saw that she was standing at the head of a flight of metal stairs. Below she could hear the faint rumbling of the furnace.

She gnawed on her lower lip and decided she should stay there for a while if the dean decided to check for her—assuming he was really after her this time. So she took the stairs down to the basement's concrete floor and stared in amazement at the size of the heating system, the massive pipes and ducts, and the empty cartons and crates stacked against the walls.

I could get lost down here, she thought as she moved to her right. It's like a secret kingdom or something. For a brief moment fascination replaced her feeling of unease.

She remembered Borden Overbrook telling her once that he'd been down there—though why, he hadn't said—and he had laughed about finding nothing more interesting than some rather ugly spiders.

Steam hissed somewhere in the back of the huge room. Pipes clanked.

With a glance back up at the door, she moved toward the rear, knowing there had to be another way out. The custodians would have to have an outside exit; that was only common sense.

But the lights, naked bulbs caged in wire mesh, were widely spaced and dim, and as she moved along an aisle formed by pieces of what looked like discarded machinery and boxes of cleaning materials, she couldn't help thinking that someone else was down there.

There were no windows that she could see.

The air was uncomfortably warm and filled with the smell of fuel oil and dust.

And above her she could hear the muffled tramping of feet as the school went about its business.

"Dumb, Field," she muttered, running a finger along the top of an empty crate. "You've really done it this time."

She was committed now to finding another exit, because if she used the upstairs hall door, and if the dean was still there, she couldn't very well tell him she'd gotten lost on her way to the administration building.

The way ahead was blocked by a man-high pile of old newspapers bound together with wire. She turned left and squeezed between a bucket of slimy water with a mop beside it and some upended planks whose tops rested against the highway of heating ducts that ran along the ceiling. The aisle she found herself in was flanked by metal shelves nearly seven feet high. Tools, rags, and boxes and bottles of cleaning powders and fluids filled up the spaces not occupied with cartons.

It was darker.

When she looked over her shoulder, she could no longer see the stairs.

When she looked ahead, she saw only the dull metal sides of a pair of huge boilers.

And she froze when she heard something moving behind them.

Her first thought was to forget about the dean and getting caught and just make her way to the stairs and leave. If he was there, she would think of something; if he wasn't, she'd just run out as fast as she could.

But as she started to retreat, she heard another sound—a groan.

She shook her head.

It was her imagination.

She shook her head again, more vigorously.

It was the middle of the day, but down there among the shadows and machinery, with the muffled roar and grumblings of the boilers, she couldn't trust what she thought she had heard. Everything was working on her imagination. A groan could only mean that someone was down there with her, and he might be hurt.

Or it might be an alien, pretending to be hurt.

Reaching blindly behind her, she grabbed the mop and held it defensively across her chest.

The envelope in her pocket grew heavy when she became aware of it, and she decided that as soon as she discovered what was or wasn't in the cellar, she'd open it and see what she had found.

A sound—something, someone, shifting.

Another groan, quieter, as if someone was trying not to be heard.

Go back, she told herself.

And cocked her head as she moved slowly forward, sidling to her left in order to get around the nearest boiler, large and square and with a bit of paint that showed it might have been green when new.

Steam hissed from a leaky valve.

A sudden belch of roaring as the other boiler blasted on and set the pipes ringing.

Jennifer swallowed, readjusted her grip on the mop, and hurried down the aisle now formed from stacks of varying lengths of discarded splintered lumber. When she reached the end, she found herself at a cinderblock wall, and she squeezed around the wood to the right and saw the far corner directly ahead, hidden in deep shadow because the bulb there was out and because it was partially blocked by a screen of tall cartons.

The first boiler was now directly on her right, its back wall blackened, its great arms reaching upward and out to connect with the ducts that either stretched to other parts of the cavernous room or vanished into the ceiling.

Condensation dripped into a pail.

There was a stool beside the boiler's door, a shovel lying beside it.

She held her breath and listened.

The dripping water sounded like coins being dropped on a hollow drum.

Keeping her eye on the corner, she edged toward the boiler, the wood at her back. Grit crunched beneath her feet. A strand of cobweb spun slowly across her face. The mop grew heavy, and she held it closer, a feeble weapon but better than nothing at all.

The boiler rambled at her.

She knew from the undisturbed layers of dust that the custodians seldom went back there. The system was automatic and probably needed tending only when something was wrong. She was straining, however, to hear the noise again.

Finally she had moved so she was standing between the two giant boilers, seeing nothing but shadow to the far wall, hearing nothing but the stream, the flames, and the thunder of her own heart.

Go, Jen! something warned her then. Go, now, before it's too late.

But she had taken only one step when she heard the rustling ahead in the dark.

Rats? she wondered and shuddered.

And then, as she continued to stare and her vision adjusted, she saw something moving, back by the wall. It was too large to be a rat, too large for any animal that might have been trapped down there. She licked her lips nervously and flattened herself against the back wall, licked her lips a second time, and sidled toward the corner.

Halfway there she stopped.

The figure she had seen was crawling along the wall, and her eyes widened when she recognized him.

"Dr. Overbrook!" she cried.

And Borden Overbrook looked up and lifted a hand in weak greeting before collapsing to the floor.

Seven

"HAS IT ONLY BEEN A COUPLE OF DAYS?" OVERBROOK asked in weary amazement. "It feels like years."

They were still in the basement, sitting on a pile of musty old rags in one corner, hidden from the rest of the room by a screen of cartons. Jennifer, after recovering from the shock of seeing her ecology instructor alive, had thrown the mop aside and run to him. He was conscious, but because of his weight it took her several minutes to help him to the bedding he had gathered for himself, and a few minutes more before she was able to help him to sit up against the wall.

"Well," he had said hoarsely, "we meet again, Miss Field. This is getting to be a habit."

The last time she had seen him, he and Pauline Klopher had been riding his motorcycle back to the Thaler campus after they had uncovered the alien hide-out behind Ballad Hill, just past a small lake called Witch's Eye. Jennifer had been in Conrad's old car, with Conrad, Marysue, and Lee, following the motor-cycle. Someone had run the car off the road. It had been badly damaged, and by the time they had been able to continue on foot something had happened to Overbrook and Klopher.

They had found the motorcycle abandoned at the side of the road, but the instructor and the librarian were missing.

Overbrook smiled as Jennifer told him about the rest of that night and the following days. "Incredible," he said. "I can't believe you haven't said a word about what happened."

"How could we?" she asked, whispering. "So far, you and Mrs. Klopher are the only adults who know we're telling the truth. The police wouldn't believe us, and we didn't dare try to make up a story. We were—to be honest, we were too scared."

"I don't blame you. I haven't exactly been laughing myself to sleep at night either."

He was filthy. His hair and face were covered with smudges and clots of dust and grime, and his bandit's mustache looked as if it were coated with grease. His dark trousers and shirt were the same, and torn in spots. And when he wrapped himself in his black leather jacket, she could see that it was in the same miserable condition.

She remembered thinking that he had looked too young to be a visiting professor from an Ivy League school; now, she thought, he looked like a man twenty years older.

He looked away when he saw her examining him, and she touched his arm in apology. He smiled gently and explained that he and Pauline had been speeding toward campus when a car, coming out of the dark with its headlights out, cut them off. Pauline had immediately leaped from the bike and raced down a slope into the woods, but his foot had gotten snared as he tried to jump off and run at the same time. He fell. Someone, it was too dark to tell who, had grabbed him while at least two others had chased after Mrs. Klopher. There had been a fight, and Borden was just able to scramble free and vanish into the trees. He had hidden there most of the night, but when he tried to get back to his apartment in one of the faculty boardinghouses, he spotted someone watching the building.

"I am not an outdoorsman," he said ruefully. "And it was getting cold, if you remember. I didn't favor hiding in the woods all night, and I didn't know anyone in town very well, so I came to the first place I could think of—here."

Though he had suffered no broken bones or other serious injuries, something must have been wrong because he awoke the next morning with a fever. A high one. It left him too weak to do anything but hide in the corner and pray no one would find him.

He had no idea what had happened to Pauline, but, though he was worried, he didn't fear the worst. She was, he thought, a resourceful woman, and a competent one.

But Jennifer was afraid that wouldn't be enough. The aliens had so far contented themselves with merely frightening them; but when Mrs. Klopher discovered the whole reason for the aliens' being there, the picture had changed.

Now, Mrs. Klopher and all she knew were gone.

Suddenly Jennifer remembered where they were and scrambled to her feet.

"We have to get you out of here," she said. "You can't stay, and the dean wants to see me. I think it's starting, Dr. Overbrook. I really think the assault is starting."

He nodded and pushed himself up stiffly, leaned against the wall for a moment, and rubbed a hand across his face. With an effort, and a refusal of her help, he struggled into his leather jacket.

"Dr. Overbrook, look, can't I—"

He stopped her with a hand on her shoulder. "Jennifer," he said. "I think, for the time being, we can dispense with the 'doctor' stuff. Borden will be fine, though my former wife told me it did make me sound like a dairy cow."

She only nodded as she maneuvered around the cartons and looked for the exit. Borden came up behind her, put a hand against the small of her back, and guided her through the maze of aisles until they came to a series of steps in the wall. As far as she could tell, they were just opposite the staircase she had come down, and she groaned silently when she realized how she might have left without finding him. It was, she thought, about the only piece of decent luck she had had all day.

Until she remembered the envelope.

Quickly she touched her pocket to be sure it was still there, then followed the man up the stairs to a wide door at the top. He put a finger to his lips and pressed an ear against the metal, then eased the crossbar down without releasing the catch.

"We're at the back," he said. "I want you to go out first."

"But—"

"You have to! If I go, and someone sees me, it'll all be over. The one thing we don't need now is the police, and they'll definitely want to see me. I need food, a night's rest in a decent bed, and time to think. All right?"

She wanted to ask about Mrs. Klopher, but she knew that he was right. Having one adult ally was, for the moment, an overriding concern. Once he was himself again, then they could find the missing librarian. And then perhaps they could tackle Jennifer's plan for getting the police out to the woods.

"Okay," she agreed, and when he pressed the crossbar all the way down, she slipped out and acted as if she had every right to be where she was. The act, however, was wasted. To left and right, the lawn that swept down a gentle slope to the forest at the back of the campus was empty. Farther down and to the right, where the grass leveled out beside the gymnasium, a class was engaged in a game of softball. When she looked up at the Union's second story, the library windows reflected only the overcast sky.

She tapped the door twice, and when Borden Overbrook came into the open, she took his hand and without thinking led him to the back corner of the building. She looked down the gap between her dorm and the Union, and there was no one on the walkway at the front. They hurried across the gap, nearly running. Jennifer wondered if she'd have the nerve to carry out her idea.

Luck remained with them.

They reached her dormitoiy, and dashed through the fire exit and up the side staircase to the second floor. Borden Overbrook started grinning, and she told herself she was out of her mind to bring a man in there, an instructor to boot. If the school ever found out, they'd lock her up and throw away the key.

A moment, then, while she checked the hall and tiptoed to her left, to the corner where her room was.

Again their luck held, and she ran back for Overbrook and practically dragged him into the room. The door slammed. The lock turned. And she sagged against the wall while the instructor made his way to one of the room's two armchairs and dropped into it with a sigh Jennifer was sure could be heard all the way to Staines. Then he looked at the prints on the walls, the desk, the books, the view of the hills outside.

"So this is how the other half lives," he said.

Jennifer couldn't bring herself to smile. She was too uncomfortable having a man in her room, and she knew she couldn't count on keeping him hidden for very long.

"Well!" he said so loudly that Jennifer knew he was uncomfortable as well. And when she dropped onto her bed, she allowed him that smile.

"You know," Overbrook said, "what I don't understand is what you were doing in that basement. It isn't exactly the hot spot of Thaler's social life."

That was when she remembered the envelope.

Hastily filling him in on why she'd been in the library, she pulled her jacket into her lap and took the envelope from the pocket. She hefted it, turned it over, then held it up for him to see. After tossing the coat aside, she moved to the foot of the bed and tore the envelope open with trembling fingers. Inside were sheets of notebook paper folded in thirds, and when she opened them she knew that what she had in her hands were Pauline Klopher's notes.

Trying to keep her excitement in check, she spread them out on the bed and stared at them, first eagerly and then with a growing sense of dismay.

"I can't read them," she said. "Borden, I can't read them!"

She handed one page to the instructor, who frowned at it and wiggled his fingers until she gave him the rest of the sheets.

"Can you make anything out of them?"

"I'm not sure," he said distractedly. "They're in a kind of shorthand—some words, some abbreviations, and the rest is symbols. It must be a private code. Tell you what," he added. "I'll try to make this stuff out if you'll be an angel and get me something to wash this garbage off my face. I feel like I've just been rescued from the gutter."

Jennifer agreed, grabbed two washcloths from her dresser, and unlocked the door. After a check of the hall she raced down to the shower room, soaked both cloths, and snatched up a bar of soap someone had left on one of the basins. On her way back she heard laughter on the front stairwell and broke into a run, slamming the door behind her with such force when she reentered her room that Borden jumped to his feet and looked as if he were about to leap out the window.

"It's all right," she said after getting her breath back. "I just scared myself, that's all. Did you learn anything?"

"I'm not sure," he said as he picked up the note-paper. "But first, a little cleaning music, please."

He took the cloths and the soap and stood in front of her mirror, muttering at his reflection. Jennifer continued to scan the papers, seeing a reference here and there that she recognized: one to the Witch's Eye, and some scientific notations that made her wonder if the librarian had discovered the exact atmosphere the creatures needed in order to survive, and the woman had written "skeleton key" at least four times that Jennifer could see.

"Skeleton key," she said to herself.

"Yes," Borden answered, drying his face on one of her towels. "I saw that too."

"What does it mean?"

"I haven't the slightest idea. A skeleton key is an all-purpose key. In theory it should open any lock of a certain type."

"But what locks?"

"I don't know, Jennifer. I don't even know if she means the locks on a door or if she's speaking figuratively."

Again she tried to make sense of what she was looking at, gave up, and handed the papers back to her instructor. She could see that he was close to exhaustion, but he couldn't sleep then. That would take time. And time was the one thing they were rapidly running out of.

Time!

With a gasp she looked at her watch and realized that Marysue should have returned long ago. She explained that Beauford would be the one to get them all safely off campus.

Borden frowned. "But what about what's-her-name? Holt? Doesn't she have a car?"

"She's gone," Jennifer said as she slipped back into her jacket. "She left a while ago, and I have no idea where she is."

"So what are you—"

"Just don't move," she told him. "Wait here until I get back. Three knocks, two, and then two, okay? Don't open the door to anyone else."

Impressed, he nodded. "You do know what you're doing, right?"

"No," she admitted. "If I did, I wouldn't feel so much like screaming."

Eight

JENNIFER LEFT THE ROOM TO THE SOUND OF HIS QUIET laughter, hurried down the hall, and swore vehemently to herself when she could not rouse Marysue. If Beauford doesn't get back here with the car pretty soon, she thought as she ran to the front stairs, taking them down two at a time, I don't know what I'll do.

She hastened to the front door and glanced into the common room. Only a handful of girls, curled on the couches, reading; in the study room to the left, the tables were empty, waiting for the evening study time.

Once on the porch, she vacillated, not knowing which way to turn, which way to run. She couldn't see the entire student parking lot and could not see the tell-tale red of the Thunderbird. Nor was she able to pick out either Lee or Conrad from among the few boys who walked between the buildings.

Please! she wished silently and started for the Student Union, staying close to the posts that held up the porch and walkway roofs, in case she spotted the dean. No one spoke to her, though a few girls looked at her oddly, and by the time she reached the Union she was frantic. They *had* to be there; they just *had* to. It was almost an hour since Marysue had left for town, and even though she wasn't a recklessly fast driver, it wouldn't take that long

59

to get to the garage and back, even picking up the boys along the way.

Calm yourself, she ordered. Just take it easy and use your head.

A deep breath, another, and she was about to reach for the door handle when Dean Dramon put a hand on her shoulder.

"I've been waiting for you," he said.

She couldn't find the words, couldn't create the excuse, and couldn't find a reason to delay when he began leading her toward the administration building. He said nothing. He nodded to other students, had a brief whispered word with a hurrying instructor, and all the time kept his hand on her shoulder, not obviously gripping it, but the slight pressure let her know that it would do her no good to try to get away.

A silent prayer for someone, anyone, to appear and save her, and they were through the high double doors, across the white marble floor of the foyer, and past the fan-shaped staircase. There were other open doors off the foyer through which she could see secretaries and clerks working at their desks, but none of them looked up, and she didn't bother to try to attract their attention when the man opened a dark oak door and ushered her into his office.

"Sit," he said, pointing to a black leather chair.

The room was huge, lined with shelves, and dominated by a highly polished walnut desk. Dramon sat behind it and rested his elbows on the top.

Jennifer sat on the edge of her chair, her hands clasped tightly in her lap. She found it difficult to breathe and even more difficult to keep her expression neutral, but she wasn't going to give him the satisfaction of knowing she was afraid.

"You've been in here before," he said at last.

She nodded, swallowing.

"You've been in a lot of places since we last talked, Miss Field."

It was an invitation to confess, and she was having no part of it.

The dean sat back and smiled at her, the smile of a hunter who has finally cornered his prey. "You know, I'm willing to wager that your parents have no idea what a troublemaker you are, no idea at all."

She braced herself, feeling suddenly that soon she was going to have to run.

Dramon held up his right hand in a fist, then slowly uncurled his forefinger and smiled at her again. "First, you are mixed up in some rather strange business that eventually resulted in the destruction of academy property. You even ended up in the hospital for a day or so, as I recall."

A second finger raised. "There was, as well, the business of your being involved with the death of my predecessor, whose murderer still hasn't been found. That little affair, I believe, resulted in the death of a policeman."

Jennifer, her temper overriding the fear that had settled over her like a cloak, stood slowly. The dean showed no outward reaction.

A third finger raised. "And then one night you were seen, by me, leaving one of the faculty houses. Where you had no business being. The same night, I might add, that Mrs. Klopher's rooms were burglarized and she disappeared. You were visiting Dr. Overbrook. Who is also gone.

"Very strange, Miss Field. Very strange indeed."

She took the two steps to his desk just as his hand curled back into a fist.

"The phrase is, I believe," he said, "three strikes and you're out."

Heat burned at her cheeks, flared through her stomach. Her knees locked, and her hands clenched tightly in fists at her sides. "You're not going to expel me," she said, and it wasn't a question.

"Oh, no." His eyes were flat, the corner of his mouth lifted just slightly. "There are no grounds."

She waited.

Somewhere in the building a telephone rang.

Then she said, "You're not going to kill me."

And he laughed. A soft laugh, but one that chilled her and made her back away. A soft laugh that continued as he rose to his feet and leaned on his fingertips over the desk, watching her, making her feel like the next meal for a cobra.

"Kill you?" he said. "Miss Field, no."

Caution flew. For the first time since the nightmare had begun, each was aware of what the other knew, and each knew there was no profit in pretense any longer. She was relieved because the enemy was there, in front of her, no longer hiding. And yet she was frightened, more frightened than she had ever been.

But more determined than ever to stop him and his unearthly friends.

"No," he said, "*I'm* not going to kill you. But I am going to stop you, Miss Field. You have no idea what you're up against, none at all. You may think you do, but you're mistaken." He walked around the desk and followed her step for step as she backed toward the door. "You'll be stopped, just as your friends have been."

"What?" Her eyes widened, then narrowed. "What do you mean?"

"The cavalry," he said, slipping his hands into his pockets. "I believe you were waiting for the cavalry to arrive? I think not. I think you'll find the Indians have cut them off at the pass."

Jennifer's hand rose to strike him, but he grabbed her wrist and yanked her to him, holding her other shoulder against his chest. When she looked up, she saw the contempt in his eyes. She was little more than an insect waiting to be crushed under his heel. When he felt like it. Not before.

"Now," he said, his voice low and rasping. "In the movies the bad guys offer the good guy a chance to join them. To be friends. To be on the winning team. And the good guy always refuses because he has principles—honor—and so-called right on his side."

His hand closed more tightly on her shoulder.

"That's ludicrous. You know it, and I know it. Which is why I'm not going to do the same for you. The bad guys are going to win because the good guys won't know what hit them. We're going to win, Miss Field, and you—you are going to lose it all."

There was no thinking now. No words. No negotiation. No threat.

Still staring into his eyes, she jammed her heel into his instep and pushed at the same time. He swore as he released her and hobbled a few paces back, swore again when she whirled around to throw the door open. A secretary stood in the middle of the foyer and looked at them curiously.

Dramon straightened up but didn't otherwise move.

Jennifer stepped over the threshold, looked over her shoulder, and said, "Go to hell."

Run!

The thought screamed at her as she walked calmly toward the exit, smiling brightly at the secretary who, surprised, smiled back. Jennifer opened the door.

Run!

Outside, she paused on the top step and inhaled deeply several times, fighting the urge to scream, fighting to stop the violent trembling that her muscles demanded. Then she closed her jacket and headed for her dorm, paying no attention to the occasional call of her name.

She didn't want to think about what the man had meant when he said the cavalry had been headed off if he had been referring to Marysue and the others. If he had been referring to Borden—but, no, that was impossible. No one knew where the instructor was.

Unless, she thought as she broke into an abrupt run, someone had gotten into her room while she'd gone and had gotten word to Dramon.

Impossible.

It had to be impossible.

She palmed the dorm door open and ran up the stairs.

He had to be there, he just had to be.

Several girls were hanging around in the hall, leaning against the wall and gossiping. They grinned as she rushed past them, called out to her as she unlocked her door and slipped into the room.

It was empty.

She gasped when the closet door opened and Overbrook stepped out.

"You forgot the secret knock," he scolded her lightly. "I didn't know who . . . Jennifer, what's the matter?"

She stood still, trying to maintain her composure. But she couldn't. Instead she flung herself into the man's arms and began to sob, hating herself for what she thought was weakness, yet unable to do anything about it. She felt his arms enfold her, gingerly, and a hand nervously patted her back while she wept. And even as the tears flowed, she couldn't help a brief smile when she wondered what Lee would think if he could see her then.

Less than a minute later it was over, and Borden moved away from her as if embarrassed. He fussed with Mrs. Klopher's notes while Jennifer dried her eyes, and he dropped into a chair when he heard what Dramon had just told her.

"They must be ready," he said grimly. "He wouldn't be so foolish as to come out in the open if he wasn't sure they were ready to begin the change."

"Then what do we do?" she asked, struggling to keep her panic from taking over.

"First, we find out what happened to Miss Beauford and Lee. If there's something we can do, we'll help them. Then we'll carry on with your plan."

"But how can we?" she asked.

"We have no choice, Jennifer," he said as he stood. "It's either that or watch them succeed."

He looked at her.

And Jennifer knew he was right.

He raised an eyebrow.

She nodded, turned, and was about to unlock the door to check the hall when someone knocked.

Borden immediately ducked into the closet, winking at her before he disappeared. When Jennifer opened the door, Monica Holt burst in and said, "Jen, you just are not going to believe what's happened now."

Nine

MONICA DIDN'T GIVE JENNIFER A CHANCE TO PROTEST. She grabbed her arm and dragged her into the hall.

"Honestly," Monica said, "it's unbelievable. Come *on,* Jen. What's the problem?"

Jennifer, whose mind was slowly switching tracks, only looked back at her room.

"Sorry, forgot about the door," Holt said, turning to close it. "But you should see—"

She stopped.

Jennifer stood behind her and put a hand to her mouth when she saw Borden's jacket lying on the floor beside the desk.

"Well," Holt said, "what have we here?" She crossed the room and picked up the jacket. Holding it in front of her, she grinned. "I don't think this is your size, Field."

All Jennifer could say was, "Where have you been, Monica? I've been looking for you all day."

"Had to go into town" was the answer as Monica held the coat up to the light. Her fur jacket made the leather look incredibly shabby by comparison, and when she finally dropped it onto the bed, it was with a grimace of distaste. "But don't change the subject."

"What subject?"

Monica pointed. "The coat, Field. It isn't yours, it sure isn't mine, and we know Miss Marysue Beauford wouldn't be caught dead in it." The grin returned. "Field, are you hiding a man in here?"

Jennifer stiffened. "Right. I've got a whole platoon of them in the closet."

"Well, you'd better get them out," Monica said, crossing her arms over her chest. "Because you're gonna need them, believe me."

"For what?"

Monica closed her mouth and shook her head.

"Monica!"

"The coat first."

Jennifer considered for a moment. Then she closed and locked the door to the room. "Okay. You win."

Holt gaped. "You mean . . ." And she looked at the closet door.

Which opened to admit Borden.

"Oh. Oh, no," Monica whispered.

"Excuse me," Borden Overbrook said, leaning in front of her to pick up the coat and slip it on. "Jennifer, we have things to do."

Monica only stared.

"And, Miss Holt, it seems that we can use your help."

It took a few seconds for Monica to get over the shock of seeing the instructor, especially in the condition he was in. But when she realized they were waiting for her, she said, "Yes! Of course. We'll—but where have you been, Dr. Overbrook?"

"That's a long story," he replied and pointed to the door. "Would you mind?"

She nodded quickly. "Right. Yes. Jennifer, I thought I had big news but—" She ran to the door, opened it, and poked her head out. Someone yelled something at her, and she yelled back while, at the same time, waggling a hand behind her to warn the others to be ready to run. Then, suddenly, she flung the door all the way open and said quietly, "Run to the fire stairs!"

Jennifer was out instantly, and Borden was right behind her. They ran up the hall and slammed into the emergency stairwell, taking the steps as rapidly as they could, using the banister to propel themselves until, panting and gasping, they reached the bottom. Monica was not far behind.

"Now what?" Overbrook asked, his expression weary and amused at the same time.

Monica wrestled the fire exit open, looked out, and glanced back at Jennifer, saying, "The gate."

Jennifer nodded her understanding, and when the signal was given she pushed Overbrook into the open and led him at a dead run across the lawn. Beyond was a heavy stand of evergreens between the lawn and the high brick wall that ran along three sides of the academy's ground. Once into the trees, she made her way to the wall and along it for several yards until she came to an old iron gate that she and the other girls sometimes used to go through to sneak off campus.

The rusted hinges complained as the trio pushed through.

On the other side were more trees and underbrush that had lost many of their leaves to the turning autumn season. They followed a narrow path to the left, almost paralleling the road until they caught a glimpse of Monica's white Mercedes parked on the shoulder.

Jennifer paused, puzzled by where the car was parked, but there was no time for questions. They dove inside and were moving almost before the doors were closed.

Borden stretched himself out on the backseat as best he could and closed his eyes.

Jennifer said, "Now, what's going on, Monica? Don't tell me Marysue got picked up for speeding."

"Worse."

"Worse? Marysue?"

"Yeah. She's being questioned as an accessory."

Jennifer squirmed until she was leaning back against the door, glancing into the back to see if Borden was all right. He was. He was resting, his eyes closed, but his lips were so tight they were nearly bloodless.

"Accessory to what?" Jennifer asked.

"Robbery. Actually, robberies."

Jennifer covered her eyes with one hand and massaged her temples. This couldn't be happening. First Lee and now Marysue. And all of it in one day. She couldn't imagine what would happen next.

"Tell me about it," she said in a small voice.

"That's all I know," Monica said, speeding down the curving road toward Staines Valley. "I was in the Hilltop having a late lunch when I heard some kids talking. At first I thought it was someone else, but when they mentioned the T-bird I knew it could only be Beauford."

"What about Lee and Conrad?"

"I don't know. I stopped at Conrad's house, but no one was home."

She said nothing more about Lee, and Jennifer knew why. From the first day they had all met, Monica had insisted the boy was trouble. He wasn't "right" for Jennifer, meaning that because his father ran a hardware store and he himself took classes at Thaler on a scholarship, he didn't belong.

What Monica forgot was that Jennifer was at the school on a scholarship too.

"It's just like this morning, y'know?" Jennifer said, rubbing hard at the back of her neck.

"I'm not surprised about Beauford," Holt continued. "I'm sure she didn't do anything, but she can get herself into more trouble just by opening her big mouth. But not to worry. It's only Rumbel being a pain again."

"How can you not worry?" Overbrook said from the backseat. "Something like that isn't the same as being cited for a traffic violation."

"I know," Monica answered impatiently. "But this guy, Rumbel, he's only blowing smoke, that's all. He already did it to Lee."

"I heard," Overbrook said.

Monica swore then as she yanked the steering wheel over, barely avoiding a gleaming black pickup that had drifted into her lane. She sounded the horn angrily and glared at the other driver.

Jennifer held her breath.

Overbrook calmly suggested that the girl not be in such a hurry.

Monica glared at him in the rearview mirror but said nothing. She concentrated on getting into and through town as fast as she could, squealing defiantly into a parking space half a block from the police station. They couldn't park behind the station because Borden might be seen. Monica leaped out of the car as though she were going to attack the station single-handedly.

Jennifer got out more slowly and looked into the back. Borden told her that he'd remain behind. She nodded and followed Holt into the same room they'd been in that morning.

And the same sergeant was there behind the counter. When he saw Jennifer he greeted her with a smile; when he saw Monica, incongruous in her fur jacket and baseball cap, he frowned.

"What can I do for you now?" he asked Jennifer.

"Marysue Beauford."

"Ah." He leaned forward on his elbows. "Well, this time I've bad news, I'm afraid. It looks as if she's going to be here for a while."

"But she didn't *do* anything," she protested tearfully.

"I wouldn't know," he said, his expression sympathetic. "I just work—"

"Sergeant Easton," Monica interrupted coolly, "does she have an attorney present?"

"She hasn't been arrested or booked," Sergeant Easton told her, just as coolly.

"It doesn't make any difference, and you know it. She still has the right to an attorney, and she'd better have one or someone's going to pay for false arrest, abridging a woman's civil rights, and—"

Easton looked away from Monica to Jennifer. "If you want to wait here, it's okay with me. But I think you'd do better coming back later."

"Later?" Jennifer asked, looking at the clock on the wall behind him. "It's close to five now. How long—"

"I don't know," he said, courtesy clearly giving way to impatience. "I'm not on the case, as you can see." And he walked away and through a door under the clock.

"I'll have his job," Monica muttered as they went back into the hall. "I'll have his badge."

"Monica, calm down, okay? This isn't going to do us or Marysue any good."

With her hands clenched helplessly at her side, she looked down the length of the brightly lit hall, wondering where Marysue was being kept and wondering, too, what they could do if they found her. They certainly couldn't run away with her. She turned and said to Monica, "C'mon, let's go."

"Go? Go where?"

But Jennifer just said they should return to the car and explain to Borden what they'd been told. He nodded thoughtfully from his prone position on the backseat and stared at the roof of the car.

"All right," he said at last. "Monica, I need some clothes, and I don't have any money. Do you have plastic?" She nodded, and he rattled off his shirt and trouser size and, after a rueful look down at his feet, his shoe size. He didn't care what he looked like, as long as he didn't look like a tramp. Then, after Monica left, he asked Jennifer to run to the nearest luncheonette or fast-food place and get him a hamburger or two. "I don't want to keel over from hunger," he said with a wan smile. "And I'm going to need more strength than I have."

Jennifer had a few dollars in her pocket, and she climbed out hurriedly and ran up the block. A coffee shop was the first place she came to, and she ordered three hamburgers and a coffee. While she waited, she stared blindly out the window to the street.

Was it only coincidence, she wondered, that Jack Rumbel was coming down so hard on them at the same time that Dean Dramon felt confident enough to openly show his hand?

And if not, was Rumbel one of them? Or was he just working for them? The latter seemed to be the most logical since Conrad had told her Rumbel had grown up in this town.

But that didn't help her current situation.

The man behind the counter spoke to her then, and she paid him, picked up the food in the white paper bag, and left.

Almost back at the car, she stopped.

There, across the street just in front of the park's wall-like hedge, was Jack Rumbel, in his cheap suit and with his large cigar. She felt her mouth open in surprise.

He wasn't alone.

He was talking to Conrad Chang, and he had the boy firmly by the arm.

Ten

A FULL MINUTE PASSED WHILE JENNIFER tried to figure out what to do. She rested behind a tree because she didn't want to be seen. She glanced over every so often and saw Conrad resisting. Not pulling or yelling, but his stance made it clear that he wasn't going anywhere.

She hurried away to the car.

She flung open the door, handed the bag to Overbrook after she climbed in, and was pleased to see Monica sitting smugly behind the wheel.

"Drive," Jennifer told her.

"What?"

"Do as I say! Drive. Turn around, and head back the other way. Don't stop until I tell you."

Monica looked at her in astonishment before nodding solemnly and doing as she was asked. Jennifer looked in the back, saw that Overbrook was changing, and looked hurriedly to the front again. She told them what she had just seen and asked Monica to pull up just before they reached Conrad.

"Why?" the girl asked as she swung the Mercedes around. "You gonna grab him or what? Is this going to be real kidnap stuff?"

"Do you have a better idea?"

"No, but I'll tell you one thing—you're not going to do it with this car, lady. Suppose that guy shoots or something? We could get killed. He could put a hole in my car, for crying out loud."

Jennifer couldn't believe that Monica would put the appearance of her automobile ahead of Conrad's freedom, but after a minute Monica did pull over, several yards short of where the two men were still standing.

"Borden?" Jennifer asked.

He had exchanged his dirty clothes for a plaid flannel shirt and jeans. Though his face was still covered with dried scratches and he badly needed a shave, he was at least less of a mess than he had been.

"What about Marysue?" he asked. "If you go ahead with what you're thinking you'll be leaving her behind. Did you see her car in the lot behind the station?"

Jennifer nodded.

"All right, then she's still in there." He slammed a hand in frustration against the back of the seat and shook his head. "I don't know. I'm sorry, Jen, but I don't know what to tell you."

For several minutes, then, they watched Rumbel. And Jennifer wasn't surprised that the man hadn't been able to budge her friend. Conrad was tall and muscular, looking even bigger now in his sheepskin coat, and though he seemed to be speaking softly it was evident by the expression on his face that he was giving the detective no satisfaction at all. And at one point, he shook off the fat man's grip.

Rumbel took out his cigar and stared at it, stared at Conrad, and shook his head.

"Well?" Monica said impatiently.

"I'm thinking!" Jennifer retorted.

"Well, think fast, Field. If he sees us, we're dead."

Suddenly Borden slid across the seat, opened his door, and said to Jennifer, "Get over to the station now and find Marysue." He lifted a hand in brusque warning when she started to protest. "If we're gone when you come out, start walking around the corner and down the street. Don't run. Walk. We'll pick you up. If Marysue wants her car, tell her to forget it for now. She'll have to wait." He climbed out and said to Monica, leaning in her window, "Get ready. You may have a whale of a driving test in a couple of minutes."

And he was gone, strolling with his hands in his pockets toward Conrad and the detective.

Monica glared at him with her arms folded.

I don't believe it, Jennifer thought as she strode to the station. What's bothering her? Can't she see we need her.

Jennifer took a deep breath and blew it out explosively; she licked her lips, chewed for a second on the inside of her cheek, and told herself it was going to be all right as long as she didn't panic. Borden knew what he was doing. Monica wouldn't let them down.

It was going to be all right.

Nothing was going to go wrong.

Jennifer hurried up the stairs of the station and almost barreled into Marysue walking out the front door. Turning back to watch the scene across the street, Jennifer hushed Marysue. "Just look," she said.

They watched as Borden Overbrook approached the detective from behind. Jennifer could tell when Conrad spotted him because his eyes widened momentarily before his expression went completely blank. Then Borden, after looking over his shoulder, stepped up to Rumbel from the rear and laid a hand on his right arm.

The detective turned and looked quickly at him, yanked the cigar from his mouth, and did nothing when Conrad broke into a run and headed for the car.

Conrad yanked the back door open and slid in, his face damp with perspiration in spite of the cold, and his blond hair tangled from his running.

Overbrook was walking quickly back toward the car; the detective remained where he was, fists at his side.

Jennifer could see Monica's fingers nervously drumming on the steering wheel, and as soon as Borden opened the door and was in, Monica shot out of the parking space and into the traffic.

Jennifer and Marysue walked swiftly down the stairs and to the curb as Monica was spinning the wheel and making a loud, smoking U-turn. Jennifer knew it wouldn't take Rumbel long to get to the station, and once he did, it was all going to hit the fan.

Borden must have asked Conrad to slide over and be ready because, as the girls ran toward the car, Conrad opened the door, leaving enough room for them to jump in.

"Go!" Borden said then, slapping Monica's shoulder. "Head for the school."

Monica sped down the street and around the next corner, using the back streets to stay away from the main road as long as she could. Twice she ran stop signs, and once she was forced to stomp on the brakes when a pair of children chased a ball into the road. But she didn't stop.

They all listened as Borden filled the others in on what had happened to him since Conrad had last seen him. Conrad explained that he'd only had ecology that afternoon at Thaler, and since the class wasn't meeting he hadn't gone. He'd gone to the park, and out of nowhere Rumbel had accosted him when he was leaving.

"He wanted to know where Lee was. I told him I didn't have any idea. Then the creep started making noises about taking me in for questioning about some stupid robbery or other, and I got so mad that I told him to call our lawyer and make arrangements for a meeting. He didn't like that."

Marysue sat quietly, holding his hand and watching him intently as he told his story. Jennifer looked over and saw that Marysue had been crying—her eyes were slightly red and puffy, and her makeup was smeared where she had wiped her cheeks.

"Are you okay?" she asked her friend.

Marysue nodded but sniffed when Conrad put his arm around her shoulders.

"I am going to sue," she said then, very slowly, her Virginia accent heavy. "I am going to take every one of them to court and make them pay for what they did. They are not going to get away with this."

"Did they touch you?" Conrad asked angrily. "They didn't hurt you, did they?"

She shook her head, smiling as quickly as she'd been close to tears. Conrad had always been solicitous, more so because he couldn't believe a girl like Marysue could be interested in a guy like him, a half-breed—his intentionally misused word for the fact that though his hair was blond and he was tall, his features, especially his eyes, were a distinct legacy from his Chinese grandfather. An odd combination, and one that obviously attracted Marysue.

"That fat slob just kept asking me questions about you and Lee. Over and over again. Like I was married to you.

I tried to tell him I wasn't your mother, but he just—"
She inhaled slowly. "He just kept coming at me. Then all
of a sudden, he stopped. Just like that."

"He was talking about me?" Conrad said in astonishment. "You mean they honestly think I had something to
do with those robberies too? I thought Rumbel was just
harassing me."

Borden turned and exchanged a worried glance with
Jennifer, but had no opportunity to say anything.

Monica was now speeding up the slope toward Thaler.
The valley had slipped away. The two-lane highway was
soon enclosed by a high wall of trees, falling away down
the hill on one side and climbing Ballad Hill on the
other. The sun was nearly gone behind the far peaks, and
shadows ranged across the blacktop.

The wind came up briefly.

There were no stars yet.

"It's no coincidence," Jennifer said, answering her own
earlier speculation. "Conrad, Marysue, Lee. And then
Dramon calls me in to threaten me. So far the only one
who hasn't been harassed is Monica."

"Good for me," the girl grumbled. "They must be going
in alphabetical order or something."

Jennifer didn't hear her. She was thinking that she
didn't know who had called Monica that morning. Maybe
they shouldn't trust the girl. Her head started to swim.
To confront her, or not? And then suddenly she remembered that no one had tried to get in touch with Lee, to
let him know what was going on. There hadn't been time.
It had all happened so swiftly, and she promised herself
to call him the moment she was able to get to a telephone.

The brick wall of Thaler suddenly appeared through
the trees.

She felt abruptly uneasy. And as Monica started to make the turn between the pillars, Borden grabbed her arm and told her to stop.

"Oh—great," Marysue said.

There, along the top arch of the drive, were two patrol cars, and a policeman was standing in front of the Student Union, talking with Peter Dramon.

Eleven

THEY KNEW THE COPS WEREN'T THERE FOR THEM because there hadn't been time for Rumbel to raise the alarm. Also, they hadn't been passed on the only road from Staines. But they were spooked anyway, and Borden ordered Monica to swing around and drive off past the school. She didn't slow until the brick wall was replaced by thick forestland. Then they continued down the sloping road. She waited until the school had curved out of sight behind her, then waited for another mile before pulling off onto the shoulder.

With the engine turned off there was a great, empty silence no one seemed able to fill.

"Well, we have them right where we want them," Monica said, breaking the quiet. "All we have to do is get them to chase us, and we can lead them right to the bad guys." Her short laugh was bitter. "Wonderful."

Borden shook his head and climbed out of the car, shivering in the shadows that stretched across the road. The others soon joined him, huddling together and staring unseeing up and down the hill, at the trees, everywhere but at one another.

Overbrook, his hands in his pockets and his arms clamped tightly to his sides, walked a few paces up the road and back again. "You know," he said thoughtfully, "Monica's idea is what Jen has wanted to do all along."

Conrad, his arm protectively around Marysue, looked puzzled until he was filled in on Jennifer's idea. For a moment he looked shocked, but when it passed he looked behind him into the woods and grunted. "We don't have much to lose, when you think about it."

"Oh, we don't?" Monica said. "Really? Well, how about this, Mr. Chang—if we go ahead with this madness and we do get those cops to chase us into the woods, and we do manage to keep away from them long enough to get them wherever we're supposed to lead them, what happens if the aliens have moved on? What happens if they're not there?"

She waved an angry hand to keep anyone from answering.

"I'll tell you what happens. We get arrested, that's what. We get arrested, and they call our parents. We get expelled even though we're not guilty, we don't graduate, and you can kiss every diploma from here to the end of our lives goodbye. That's what happens."

And she stalked off up the road, kicking at stones, swiping at the air, and not looking back when Marysue called her name.

"What's gotten into her?" Marysue wanted to know. "I would have thought she'd think it was a good idea."

"Not when she thought it through to the consequences," Borden said as he watched her pick up a rock and throw it into the trees as hard as she could. "I think she didn't believe it would come to this."

"But she has a point about the aliens moving off," Conrad said reluctantly.

"Yeah. I know."

"Then we can't wait around here, can we?" Jennifer told them. "We have to go to the Witch's Eye right now and see if the aliens are still there." When they looked at her as if she'd suggested a quick trip to the moon and back, she shrugged. "We don't have a choice, do we?"

Monica stomped back down the road and heaved herself into the front seat without saying a word.

The drive to the lake was made in silence.

Monica followed Overbrook's terse instructions to the barely visible trail off the road. It wasn't much wider than the car, and if she hadn't been told it was there she would have driven right past it.

Swearing but not balking, she pulled the car onto it and winced every time a low-hanging branch or shrub scraped against the sides and the roof. Shortly afterward, they saw two huge boulders, and the trees fell away beyond them to form a clearing. Left and right were two ramshackle cabins, and directly ahead was a small body of water, part of its surface covered with colonies of green algae.

Witch's Eye.

Now reflecting only the darkening sky, it rippled as the night's first wind blew slowly across it.

At Overbrook's direction, Monica stopped the car just before the boulders. Then they climbed out and again stood close together, moving toward the clearing.

"I don't suppose anyone thought to bring a flashlight," Conrad said as he looked into the woods.

The light was failing swiftly, and Jennifer felt as if she were peering through a thin black veil. She closed her jacket to the neck and put her hands in her pockets, wishing there could at least be a moon to give them something to see by. But there was only the faint glow of the clouds as the sun set behind them, and an even fainter reflection in the water.

Jennifer looked at Conrad and Marysue and wished Lee were with her. She was strong, but she didn't want to be alone, not then.

Besides, she thought, this wasn't the way it was supposed to be. They were going to have a plan, step by step, all aspects of the problem covered and readied.

The way they were proceeding now was like running full tilt into a dark room—having no idea of what was in there, not knowing if anything had been changed while they were gone.

They could make it safely to the other side, or they could trip and break their necks.

"Well, I'm tired of standing around here freezing," Monica said. "If one of you will show me the way, I'll scout the Indian camp and bring back a scalp."

She made no attempt to hide the disgust in her voice, but no one rose to the bait. Borden Overbrook suggested that they not all go, because if they were spotted someone had to be left to get away and bring help. The discussion that followed was conducted in whispers, harsh and rapid. They finally concluded that Borden was still too weak to do any running; he argued but was overruled.

Conrad said he'd go, shaking his head when Marysue instantly volunteered to go with him. "Two will make enough noise," he told her gently. "Three, and we'll sound like an army."

"I don't like it, Zucco," Beauford told him.

"I'm not so crazy about it myself," he admitted. "But there it is, Richmond."

And before Monica lost her temper again at what she obviously thought was their stalling, he took her elbow and led her quickly away, bending his head to talk to her as they moved off to the right, past the cabin and onto a trail Pauline Klopher had shown them a few days before.

Marysue walked slowly back to the car.

Borden shivered and politely refused Jennifer's offer of her coat. "I'd split the seams, but thanks anyway. I think Marysue has the right idea. We should wait in the car. It'll be warmer, and we'll be able to see anyone coming along the trail."

The windows were down.

Jennifer heard an owl, heard the wind rattling the branches of the mostly bare trees, heard water slapping against a rock on the lake's shore.

She also heard Marysue in the backseat, trying valiantly not to let them know she was crying.

It was full dark.

As if in answer to Jennifer's prayer, the clouds began to shred, and silver light began to filter into the clearing.

"Skeleton key," Borden said, and Jennifer jumped.

"What's that?" Marysue asked, invisible in the darkness in the back.

He told her about Pauline's notes. As Jennifer's eyes adjusted to the gloom, she saw his profile—pensive, almost sad.

"While you and Monica were getting me the food and clothes," he said to her, "I figured out what she was talking about on those papers." He took a slow breath and shook his head. "I still find it hard to believe, you know. But—the skeleton key is what the aliens need to transform it all. Remember those plants we saw, what Zucco—what an odd nickname, don't you think?—said about them, that it looked as if they hadn't been burned but withered?"

Jennifer nodded, and Marysue shifted until her fore-arms were resting on the back of the seat and her chin was propped up on her wrist.

"Genetic engineering," he continued. "It's what they're doing. Instead of plants giving off oxygen, our friends from Alpha Centauri, or wherever, want them to give off something else. But to do that, they have to find the genetic key for every different species they need to alter. The skeleton key is something that would alter them all, whether they're dealing with redwoods or plankton."

Jennifer closed her eyes for a moment, trying to imagine how it could be done and knowing she couldn't because it was well over her head. "The notes," she said then. "Did Mrs. Klopher know if they—"

"Succeeded?" Borden shrugged. "She could only make an educated guess."

"So what did she guess?" asked Marysue.

"Almost."

"No!" Marysue whispered.

Jennifer closed her eyes briefly, knowing that the chill spreading along her spine had nothing to do with the weather outside.

"It's a nitrogen-based atmosphere," Borden went on, seemingly oblivious to the effect he was having on the girls. "That means the preliminary changes could be made without our knowing it. Until it was too late."

"You mean," Marysue said, "we could breathe that stuff?"

"No. We couldn't. If they find what they're looking for, and they start the changes, we'll never know what hit us. It would be like—it would be like walking down the street and strangling to death without anyone touching you."

Jennifer straightened. That, she thought, is why the aliens are so active now. They may not have the key yet, but they are close enough to feel confident. Which explained why Dramon had openly confronted her, and why she and her friends were being harassed—the aliens wanted them out of the way. And it was still better for them to do it through the law—and especially through a cop who hated kids—than through outright murder.

That will come when they're finished.

"Tonight," she said aloud.

Marysue looked at her. "What?"

"Tonight," she repeated. "If we do this right, with Borden on our side, we can end it tonight."

Marysue grunted. "And I bet you still believe in Santa Claus."

Jennifer guessed that nearly an hour had gone by. She was getting cold and decided it would be easier to wait and get warm by walking around. She slipped out of the car and walked around it, staring in the direction Conrad and Monica had gone, staring back at the trail, and straining to listen for the sound of pursuit.

Something small and dark streaked across the dark water, and Jennifer had to clamp a hand to her mouth to stop herself from screaming when Marysue crept up beside her.

"You okay?" Jennifer asked.

"I'll live. But I'm still gonna sue."

They stood shoulder to shoulder, sharing their warmth, sharing their wavering strength.

"You know Overbrook?" Marysue said quietly.

"What about him?"

"All this stuff he said—it scared me to death."

"I know."

"Do you think he's right?"

Jennifer shrugged. "I have to think so. He's the expert we were looking for. He knows more about this than we do."

Marysue sighed out loud. "I wish you hadn't said that, Field. I was hoping you were thinking he was full of it."

"I wish he was."

They turned to face the car. Borden Overbrook was still inside, but they couldn't see him. Jennifer looked away—it was like looking at a ghost, and she didn't like it.

"It's been too long," Marysue said as they gave up waiting by the lake. "I could have crawled there and been back long before this."

Though Jennifer was beginning to feel the same way, she didn't respond. Borden Overbrook was getting out of the car, and when she was close enough to see his face, she knew he agreed.

"The horns of a dilemma," he said. "We can't go after them because we might miss them in the dark. And if we stay here, we're going to drive ourselves crazy."

"Well, then, two of us will go, and we'll leave someone here."

"Alone?" Jennifer said.

"Well, we can't stand around here anymore," Marysue snapped tearfully. "Like the man said, it's driving—"

She stopped when Jennifer suddenly whirled around and faced the direction Conrad had taken. Someone was out there, running, crashing into the underbrush, making no attempt to hide his approach. Borden pulled them back in the direction of the car and slightly behind him, and held out his arms just in time to catch Monica, who tripped over something unseen on the ground and fell against his chest.

"What happened?" Jennifer demanded. "Where's Conrad?"

Monica gulped for air, then looked up at Borden. "Back there," she gasped. "They—they saw us. He's back there."

Twelve

MARYSUE CRIED OUT, LESS IN FEAR THAN IN ANGER, and she looked at Jennifer and said, "I've got to find him!"

Jennifer tried to stop her.

To go out there then, in the dark, with the alarm raised and the aliens knowing there were others hunting for them, was suicidal, but Beauford refused to listen. She stood for a second with her hands flapping at her sides, then bolted toward the trail.

Borden yelled at her to stop, but he couldn't move because Monica was holding on to him so tightly.

Jennifer wavered between good sense and going with her friend. It was crazy; the whole plan was falling apart. Finally, with a sigh, she cast an apologetic look at the instructor and raced away into the dark.

She could barely see.

Though the clouds were still breaking up, and the resulting starlight was better than nothing, there were still more shadows than substance. She braced herself with every step in anticipation of tripping.

The bulky silhouette of the ruined cabin was dark on her right, the lake on her left nothing more than a faint break in the trees. Ahead, she could see Marysue slow down abruptly as she searched for the trail, a short length of wood in her left hand for a club. When she came up behind her, Beauford whirled around, ready to strike, and grinned sheepishly when she saw Jennifer. Marysue told her to pick up a weapon because the creatures weren't going to be satisfied, this time, with simply scaring the girls away.

Marysue went first, sweeping the wooden board from side to side to clear the path they were following; but they hadn't gone more than a few yards when they heard something crashing through the trees toward them.

Jennifer tugged at the back of Beauford's coat, telling her they'd better retreat—at least until they found out who, or what, was coming.

Marysue balked.

Jennifer insisted, gripping her arm firmly and yanking her until they were back in the clearing. Then, as Marysue crouched down to hide, Jennifer hurried to the cabin, scanning the ground for something she could use to protect herself.

It came nearer.

Jennifer straightened up for a moment—there was more than one, but she couldn't tell if they were coming together or if one was being chased.

Suddenly the headlights of the Mercedes flared on, nearly blinding her though they weren't aimed in her direction. Its engine roared, and she could hear earth and pebbles being kicked out from under it as the automobile backed out toward the highway. She ran a couple of steps toward the departing headlights, groaned in despair, and ran back to the cabin. And there, near the concrete slab that had been used as a stoop, her foot kicked something hard. She bent down, ran her hands along it, and realized it was a poker, old and rusted but still heavy enough to do damage.

Footsteps made her leap to her feet, the poker at her shoulder like a baseball bat.

It was Borden.

"Don't worry," he said. "I sent Monica back to get the police."

"But will they come?"

He grinned. "They will if she does what I tell her."

The thrashing was even louder, so close it was impossible to tell how many were making the ungodly noise.

Nightbirds rose complaining from their branches, and the snapping of twigs and branches made it sound as if a lightless fire was racing toward them.

Then Marysue cried out from her position by the trail and ran to the cabin, spun around when she reached Borden and Jennifer, and pointed.

They could all see it.

Lumbering toward them along the path.

It was as tall as a man, walking on two legs, yet its shape and the fur that covered it gave it the appearance of a gigantic wolf.

But it was the eyes that were the most terrifying— slanted and green, almost aglow in the starlight. And though life was there, it was life she had never known. It was cold. It was distant. It was impossible to read anything from the animal's expression save its clear intention to destroy its enemies.

The creature stopped when it saw them standing by the cabin, and a low, satisfied growl rumbled from deep in its throat. Marysue was gone. Where was she? Borden backed away a step, reached for the poker, and scowled when Jennifer refused to give it up. Instead she side-stepped a few feet away from the instructor, dividing the creature's attention, giving it a choice.

Suddenly it threw up its arms, howled, and fell face first to the ground. Marysue stood over it, clubbed it again on the back of its head, and gave the others a thumbs-up gesture.

Howling exploded from the woods.

Another one came out of the brush by the lake.

It charged straight at Jennifer just as a third one broke from the trail and managed to duck under Marysue's wild swing. Borden ran to help her while Jennifer stood her ground, watching the alien lope toward her, snarling, spitting, its eyes firmly fixed on her and not blinking once when it spotted her weapon.

It came on, and Jennifer braced herself, trying not to listen to the struggle on her right.

Then she threw herself to the left and swung one-handed, the poker slamming into the beast's side and sending it sprawling. A fierce stinging raced up her arm as she regained her balance, and she grunted, shifted the poker to her other hand, and watched the alien roll over several times before struggling to its feet.

It stood, swaying, rubbing its side and shaking its head slowly.

She inched closer, switching the poker in front of her like the tail of a cat.

Borden Overbrook bellowed in pain; Marysue screamed in rage.

Jennifer swung the poker halfheartedly, a deliberate feint to see which way the beast would jump. But it didn't move. It only watched her as it continued to rub its side. And when she swung again, its growl was almost like laughter.

Marysue shouted.

Two more creatures burst out of the trees.

Jennifer wasted no more time. She lunged with the poker, pulled back when the creature reached for it, and laid it solidly on the side of its neck. It fell to its knees, and Jennifer kicked its shoulder, lashed out again as she ran by, and charged the alien pair that were running toward Beauford.

Overbrook, having fought off the third one, threw his hands out just as one of the pair flung itself at him. They rolled over and over, grunting, snarling, and finally disappearing around the corner of the cabin. Marysue, meanwhile, was fending off the other one with what was left of her board, her hair matted over her face, one sleeve of her jacket torn from shoulder to elbow.

Jennifer, unable to get close enough to strike the creature because it was moving too quickly, screamed to distract it. The alien hesitated for only a moment, but it was enough—Marysue jammed her battered club into its midsection, which doubled it over, driving it back. Jennifer slammed its head viciously, the sickening sound of iron crushing bone loud enough to fill the clearing.

Beauford immediately dropped to her knees, panting, and Jennifer hurried to her side.

"Are you okay?" she asked, running a trembling hand along the slash of her coat.

"I—think so." Marysue leaned back on her haunches and lifted her face to the sky. "You know, I didn't really think I could do it."

Jennifer nodded her agreement and averted her eyes from the wolf-things lying on the ground. Then she turned and ran toward the back of the cabin, looking for Borden and the creature that had attacked him. But she could see nothing, not anywhere in the clearing, and no sounds reached her that would give her a clue.

Feeling her knees begin to weaken and her arms fill with lead, she staggered back to her friend and helped her to her feet.

"Overbrook?" Marysue said.

"I don't know. They're both gone." She looked into the dark, eyes straining and failing. "I don't know. Maybe he chased the thing down the road."

"Or the other way around."

Jennifer shrugged. Right then it didn't make any difference. There was nothing they could do, and their next step was to get back on the trail to look for Conrad. Beauford wasted no time, and, supporting each other like a pair of drunks, they ducked under the trees.

"He better be all right," Marysue whispered harshly.

Jennifer thought about Monica and prayed that the girl had somehow contrived to get the police to chase her back. Though a quartet of aliens were out of commission, she had no idea how many more, if any, were still back at their den.

Several times they stopped to listen but heard nothing except the ragged gasp of their own breathing.

Every few minutes the wind would kick up, and the trees would release more of their leaves. They skated off their heads and shoulders, more than once making them think they were bats. Underfoot they crackled, and the two soon gave up any pretense of being quiet.

Above them the wind blew steadily, keening through the bare branches on top of Ballad Hill.

It was, Jennifer thought, like walking through a graveyard; and she scolded herself immediately. Thoughts like that weren't going to do her any good, especially not then.

Some time later they reached a small clearing, where many of the plants and trees were dead or dying from the experiments the aliens were doing to get them to emit something other than oxygen.

The idea made her shudder.

And when Marysue grabbed her arm and pointed to the uphill edge of the clearing, she almost yelled.

There was a dark form on the ground—alien or not they couldn't tell. After listening for any signs of someone lurking beyond the reach of their vision, they separated and approached the form from two sides.

When it groaned and sat up, Jennifer brought the poker to her shoulder.

When it swore, Marysue uttered a short cry and ran to it, dropped beside it, and threw her arms around Conrad.

Jennifer waited seconds before joining them, helping the young man to his feet.

"What happened?" she asked.

"I'm not sure," he said, grinning at them somewhat weakly. "Monica and I were down there"—he pointed toward the continuation of the trail—"when we were jumped. We ran, but one of them hit me from behind when we got back here. I guess he thought I was dead. We Changs have thick skulls, you know. Anyway, the next thing I know this maniac is throwing herself all over me."

"I was not throwing myself all over you," Marysue said, only partially fighting back her tears of relief and concern.

"Whatever," Jennifer said briskly. "We can't stay here. Come on, we have to get back. Can you walk, Zucco?"

Conrad nodded, winced, and grabbed the back of his head. "Yeah," he said. "Just don't plan on doing any running."

The return to the cabin clearing was slow, and though Conrad asked several times what was going on, neither of the girls wanted to take the time to answer. Marysue told him just to wait and she'd explain everything; Conrad insisted he wasn't an invalid and had a right to know where everyone else was. By the time they were more than halfway back, Marysue had given up and tried to fill him in, but the answers came in fits and starts as they dodged fallen trees and stumbled into brush. And by the time they reached the clearing, Jennifer was sure Conrad was more confused than ever—especially about what had happened to Borden Overbrook.

"The last time I saw him was here," Jennifer said, pointing at the area between the cabin and the woods. "I don't know what happened to him after that. I looked but—"

Marysue touched her shoulder and hushed her. Pointed toward the other cabin on what would be the other side of the road.

Jennifer looked, blinked, and saw a car parked there.

And before any of them had a chance to move, the headlights came on and a voice said, "It's all over, punks. There's a gun here. Drop whatever it is you're holding, little lady, and raise your hands high."

"Wouldn't you know it," Conrad muttered. "It's Jack Rumbel."

Thirteen

SLOWLY JENNIFER LOWERED THE POKER TO THE ground, while, with her other hand, she shaded her eyes against the glare of the headlights. She could see nothing in the beams they cast, though she heard the fat detective moving across the ground and heard Conrad whispering something to Marysue as he shifted to his left.

"Shut up!" Rumbel said. And Conrad almost snapped to attention, Marysue grabbing hold of his arm with both hands and turning her face away from the light.

Oh, no, Jennifer thought, what does he need a gun for?

Then one of the headlights was blotted out by the large figure in an overcoat. The detective approached them cautiously, the leaves beneath his feet snapping like thin glass. And the closer he came the more she could make him out—from the dark open overcoat he wore with the collar up to the flapping trouser legs beneath it.

She still couldn't see his eyes, but she could see the gun and the twisting plumes of steam as the man breathed.

"It seems," Rumbel said casually, "that you have some explaining to do." He laughed, though it sounded more like a series of snorts, and moved the gun to cover Conrad. "This I gotta hear."

"Aliens," Jennifer said.

Rumbel moved closer, his left hand hanging loose at his side. "Aliens?"

"No, Jenny," Marysue whispered, and when Jennifer turned her head to tell the girl this was the perfect time to let the secret out, she realized that the aliens they had fought in the clearing were gone. She turned a tight circle, using the car's lights to show her that they all had been taken away.

"You gonna tell me," the policeman said, "there are illegal aliens here? In Connecticut? You think I'm gonna believe there are aliens up here?"

Closer still, the gun's dark metal gleaming.

She shook her head.

"Right. Wise move, little lady."

"How'd you know we were here?" Conrad asked.

"A little bird," Rumbel sneered.

"Monica—"

"Who?" The detective was less than ten feet away now, the gun aiming at no one in particular, but neither was it pointing toward the ground. "Who's Monica? Another one of your little gang? From high-and-mighty Thaler?"

Jennifer and Marysue exchanged startled glances—if Monica hadn't lured the man there, then how did he know where to find them? And what had happened to her?

And where, she thought further, is Borden?

She didn't want to think he was dead, but he'd been gone too long, and there was no other conclusion.

From his coat's deep pocket Rumbel pulled out a flashlight and shone it toward the lake, toward the cabins, swept it across the face of the trees bordering the clearing. "I don't get it," he said. "What's this place to you?"

"Nothing," said Marysue. "We just like it here."

"Really?" He laughed again and shook his head. "You kids must think I'm really stupid, huh? You come here to hang out. Walking, yet, 'cause I don't see any car or bike. No booze, no fire, not even a little smoke or two, right? You just hang out in the dark and tell each other ghost stories." He scowled and stood to one side. "Over there," he ordered, using the gun as a prod. "Over by the car. Now!"

The temptation to make a break for it was strong. Running, however, wouldn't solve anything now. Not so long as Rumbel had the gun.

Jennifer walked past without looking at him and stood by the driver's door, waiting. She watched Conrad remain beside Marysue.

Suddenly she sensed the presence of someone else nearby. Someone looking at her. She turned and peered into the backseat of the car, gasped, and whirled away when the detective pushed her gently to one side and opened the door.

"Surprise," he said flatly. "A Fawkes bird."

Lee slid out, glaring at the cop as he wrapped Jennifer in his arms, giving her a hug that took away her breath before releasing her again. "He caught me hitching out to campus," he said to Conrad's unasked question. "I had to talk to you, Jen, but Rumbel and I had the long talk."

"Indeed we did," the man said, lining them up with their backs to the lake so he could lean against the fender and watch them. "There I was, heading out to the school to find a kid who ran from me and some jerk who broke every speed limit in New England, and what do I see but this punk walking up the hill, like he didn't have a care in the world."

"How come we didn't see you?" Jennifer asked Lee.

"I don't know. I went through the woods part way," he answered.

"I picked him up and we took a ride," the detective answered. "I decided I wanted some answers without any funny stuff. Nice time of year, don't you think?"

Jennifer felt rather than saw Lee start to take a step forward, and she stopped him by slipping her arm around his waist. When he looked at her, she sighed to let him know it wouldn't do any good.

"What did you tell him?" Conrad asked.

"Everything," Lee said sullenly.

"What?" Jennifer and Marysue said together.

"Well, sure!" Rumbel said, rubbing the gun barrel along the front of his coat. "I let him know there are always options, even for punks, and I explained each one to him, very carefully."

"And you believe him?" Jennifer asked, feeling Lee nudge her with his hip too late.

"That boy," Rumbel said, making the word sound as if he were talking about the scum on the lake, "is fairly well known in my line of work, little lady. But he isn't dumb. He knows when to fish and when to cut bait." He nodded slowly. "He told, and I'm surprised you let yourselves go along with him."

Conrad's confused expression would have been comical in different circumstances, and Jennifer's mind was racing, trying to understand what was going on. Lee *hadn't* told about the aliens; he had told Rumbel something else, and she willed the others not to say anything until they knew what it was.

Something moved in the dark beyond the cabin.

Jennifer stared in that direction, looked back at the detective, who was scratching the side of his neck, and realized he hadn't heard anything.

They're coming back, she thought. Oh, no, they're coming back.

"Ev-everything?" Conrad said, the question as much for Lee as for Rumbel.

"Sure, why not?" Lee said, shaking Jennifer's arm away and facing his friend squarely. "He already knows, right? He talked to me, he talked to Richmond here for who knows how long—what's not to tell? Anyway, he said"—Lee kicked at a stone—"he said it would go better if we didn't keep trying to talk our way out of it."

"Talk our way out of *what?*" Marysue asked, nearly shouting.

"Telling him where it was."

Jennifer understood what was happening and couldn't help a quick smile that vanished as soon as Rumbel looked in her direction. Then she leaned her cheek on Lee's arm and continued the deception by saying, "I'm sorry. It was a good place."

"Not your fault," he replied, delighted that she had caught on. "The whole thing was stupid."

"Right!" Rumbel said smartly, pushing himself away from the car. "Now all I want you to do is show me where you hid all the stolen stuff. Fawkes here," he added to the others, "told me there'd be no trouble." The gun came up, resting against his chest. "I think he's right, right?"

Jennifer, trying desperately to look repentant, nodded, as did the others, who had finally caught on.

"All right, then." Rumbel looked around the clearing and wrinkled his nose. "I don't suppose we can take the car, huh?"

"No," Lee answered. "We have to walk."

"Far?"

"In the dark, half an hour, maybe more."

"Great." The detective reached through the driver's window and pulled out a microphone that snapped

static at him until he called in to the station and told
the dispatcher he would be out of service for a while.
After he had replaced the mike on its hook under the
dashboard, he straightened up, put the gun in his pocket
with his hand still around it, and used the flashlight as
a pointer.

"Go," he said. "And do me a favor, huh? Don't try to
run."

They moved in single file across the clearing, Rumbel
trailing and complaining about what a cop had to do to
make good in a hick town. And as Jennifer followed Lee
into the woods, Marysue and Conrad ahead, she understood why the detective hadn't called in another unit to
help him. Lee had convinced him that this wasn't an
ordinary series of thefts they were talking about. And a
successful completion of what, for Staines, would be a
major case, would mean promotion for the man.

Ego had led Jack Rumbel, alone, straight into Jennifer's
plan.

She heard something moving parallel to them, back in
the trees. And this time the detective heard it too,
because he paused for a moment, mumbled something to
himself, and, when she dared a glance over her shoulder,
she saw that his gun was out again.

"Friends of yours?" Rumbel asked, pointing toward
the sound.

"No," she said truthfully. "Probably just some animal."

"Great."

And he said "great" again when they reached the first
clearing and he saw the gray dying plants. "What
happened here?"

He didn't wait for an answer, however. He used the
flashlight to check the clearing's edges, then waved them

on, to the left and back onto the trail. He was panting softly now, and Jennifer prayed he wouldn't be too winded by the time they reached the den.

And she prayed that whatever was pacing them wouldn't make its move until then either. This was their chance to get someone in authority involved, even if he was a kid hater, and she wanted to be at the site before anything was done. Rumbel had to be alert. He had to be ready. Anything less, and they would all be killed.

The next clearing was even worse than the first—it was as if they had stumbled upon a lunar landscape, and she caught snatches of conversation between Zucco and Marysue, the gist of which was that the dead plants and their withered condition were evidence of the aliens' failed experiments.

But the dead areas had been so for quite some time.

Mrs. Klopher had learned that things had changed since.

Jennifer wished she knew more about genetics, because the skeleton key seemed like pure fantasy to her. How could one species, even at the cellular level, be crossed with another? It was impossible.

Impossible for us, she answered herself. But these creatures come from the stars.

"Hold it," Rumbel ordered as Conrad started out of the clearing. "Hold it a minute." And he leaned against the trunk of a still-living birch, his chest heaving, his face covered with perspiration.

"Come on," Lee said impatiently. "We can't stop now."

"Why not?" the man asked, eyeing him suspiciously. "You got a time bomb or something?"

"I just want to get it over with," Lee told him. "And I'm cold."

"Well, that's just too bad," Rumbel said. "I'm out of breath, and we're gonna wait until I get it back, you hear?"

"I don't think you will," Marysue said and pointed to the alien who had stepped out from the trees.

Fourteen

No One Moved.

Jennifer's first reaction was terror; her second was relief because finally one of the wolf-creatures had shown itself to someone else. Yet terror was the stronger emotion, because where there was one alien, there were bound to be others. And she couldn't help but listen for the sounds of more approaching.

Rumbel, whose expression had switched rapidly between amazement and disgust, finally sneered as he pushed away from the tree and drew his gun. "What's this?" he asked, aiming the flashlight directly into the alien's face. "Halloween?"

The alien stood motionless at the back of the clearing, its eyes narrowing as it took in the detective and the others. Then it snorted and moved forward. When Conrad took a step forward, it stopped him with a glare.

"Come *on,*" Rumbel said as if tired of playing games. "Is this what you were gonna show me, Fawkes? A lousy costume? Can't you do any better than this?"

Marysue covered her mouth with her hand, though not in time to prevent a soft whimper from escaping.

"It's not a costume," Lee said tonelessly.

"Lee," Jennifer said.

He gave her a look and a slight shake of his head.

She suddenly realized what he was thinking—there were five of them and only one alien. They could overpower the creature and, with luck, take it prisoner. She could feel him shifting, and she saw Conrad slowly rolling his shoulders beneath his jacket. Marysue didn't move—she was frozen to the spot, her eyes wide with fear.

The alien ignored them as it moved straight for the detective.

"All right," Rumbel said, "this has gone far enough." He raised the gun. "Stop, punk, and take off that stupid mask. This is the police."

The alien snarled.

Jennifer thought it sounded like laughter.

"It's no costume, Rumbel," Lee said again.

"You must think I'm crazy," the man said, shaking his head in disgust and pulling the hammer back.

The alien hesitated and stopped.

"Good, very good," the detective said. Then, before anyone could warn him, he closed the gap between them and grabbed a handful of the alien's hair. He pulled, and the alien bellowed, one arm sweeping out to knock the man aside.

The gun fired harmlessly into the tree.

The flashlight spun into the air, its beam whipping crazily across the boles and branches.

Lee and Conrad immediately threw themselves at the creature, riding it to the ground while it howled and thrashed about in an attempt to throw the two boys off its back.

Rumbel, who hadn't been knocked off his feet but was nevertheless stunned, shook his head to clear it and advanced on the wrestling figures. His gun was out again, but if he intended to shoot, he had no chance—the boys covered the creature too well, and he clearly didn't want to hit them.

He looked around for a moment and said "What's going on here?"

Marysue finally screamed.

Jennifer, after taking a step toward the fighters, whirled around and raced for the flashlight. She grabbed it and aimed it at the ground until she found a stout branch, which she picked up.

The alien howled.

Rumbel swore out loud.

Marysue ran to Jennifer and grabbed the branch from her hand, ran to the boys, and lifted the club over her head, ignoring the detective's orders to stand back before she got hurt.

Suddenly the alien hunched up to its hands and feet and threw out one arm. Lee was flung to one side, landed at the edge of the clearing, and rolled up against a tree. His head struck the trunk, and he grunted and went limp. Jennifer cried his name and raced to him, dropped onto the ground, and passed the flashlight beam over his face—his eyes were open, but they were glazed. She slapped his cheeks lightly.

"Lee," she said tearfully. "Lee, come on, wake up!"

Conrad was still grappling with the creature, his weight an advantage, but the alien was stronger, and it wasn't long before it had struggled to its feet, the boy clutched in its deadly embrace.

Marysue brought the club down on the alien's shoulder.

It snarled, but didn't fall; nor did it release Conrad.

"Move!" Rumbel yelled and bullied Marysue out of his way. He maneuvered himself behind the alien and threw an arm around its neck. He pulled back on his neck while stabbing the gun's barrel repeatedly into its side.

Marysue began exhorting Conrad to get out of the way so she could use her weapon.

Lee groaned and rubbed his face with one hand. But when he tried to struggle to his feet, Jennifer stopped him, whispering anxiously that he was still too groggy.

He looked at her angrily, but when he tried again, he could only moan and fall back against the trunk.

Conrad freed one arm and punched the alien as hard as he could.

Rumbel put the gun against the creature's head and said, "Stop, or I'll blow your head off."

But the alien suddenly bent its knees, straightened, and threw Conrad away, spinning and clubbing Rumbel with its forearm. The fat man stumbled back, and the alien clubbed him again, and a third time, sending the gun to the ground and the man after it. After Rumbel had regained his feet, he gaped at the creature with the first true fear he had shown.

It growled at him.

Rumbel began to tremble, sweat poured from his face, and he turned and ran back the way they had come.

Then the alien whirled again to face the others, snarling, its teeth bared and its eyes so narrowed they were nearly closed.

Marysue swallowed but didn't drop her branch.

Lee gulped for air, and Conrad barely managed to pull himself to his knees.

Jennifer couldn't think. She aimed the flashlight directly into its face and prayed the others would get back on their feet.

Then the alien said, "You," in a soft, whispering rasp.

The flashlight dropped from her hand.

The alien's lips curled into a cruel semblance of a smile. "You," it repeated.

It took a step toward her, and Jennifer looked around, searching for something she could use to hold it off. Lee pushed himself upright, fists up though he was blinking rapidly, and the alien only snarled that hideous laughter again.

"You," it said to Jennifer. "You have no place to go now."

And before any of them could move, it sprang into the underbrush and vanished.

It took them nearly thirty minutes to stagger back to the Witch's Eye clearing. Conrad was badly bruised and shaken, and Lee was still having a hard time focusing. None of them spoke. They followed the flashlight's beam until they saw the first cabin, and at a silent signal all but Jennifer fell exhausted through the battered doorway onto the floor.

She stood on the threshold and watched the Witch's Eye turn black.

A chill deeper than any winter could provoke made her hug herself.

More than anything, she wanted to wake up.

But the faint moans behind her reminded her that she was not dreaming.

"You have no place to go now," the creature had told her, and by the time she had reached the cabin she knew it was right.

Rumbel, a coward at the end, had fled, and she had no doubt he didn't believe for a second the alien was real.

Or maybe he was one of them—they hadn't tested him—and Borden Overbrook was missing again.

Even if Rumbel persuaded other policemen to go out there and search, she knew the aliens would be gone again.

They were fugitives now. All of them.

There was no one left to help them.

Lee came up behind her and slipped an arm around her waist. "It's lousy," he said, in such a way that she knew he'd been thinking all the same things she had.

"I guess," Marysue said from the dark of the cabin, "we're on our own. Right, Field?"

She turned around. "Right."

"Well, you got any ideas?"

Jennifer stared at her and suddenly began to laugh. It was the only thing she could do, because Marysue was right. They couldn't depend on anyone now; they would have to do it all themselves. They had no choices.

"All right," she said. "I guess we have to plan."

And at that the others began to laugh, close to the edge of hysteria. But the feeling in the room was clear—they wouldn't let anyone beat them.

Or anything.

And Jennifer almost allowed herself to feel as confident as she sounded. And then Lee said, "The alien."

Silence.

And the one thought none of them had wanted to bring to the surface, Lee put into words.

"The voice," he said. "It sounds dumb, but I think I recognized it."

"I know," said Jennifer. "I know. It was Monica."

www.ingramcontent.com/pod-product-compliance
Lightning Source LLC
Chambersburg PA
CBHW072006170626
46813CB00005B/2029